The

RUNESTONE

"Them Boys Was Here Alright!"

By

Ralph A. Mayer

This book is dedicated to:

JEANE LEWIS SIMPSON

With my greatest thanks for her continual love, example and inspiration.

Published by Fivecoats Publishing Co.
31524 510th Ave.
Ottertail, MN 56571

Published, bound and printed in the United States of America.

First printing   2008

ISBN Number – 0-9774028-1-9
ISBN13 Number – 978-0-9774028-1-6

Library of Congress – Registered 2008   #TX0006867175

Acknowledgements

Saying 'thank you' seems so inadequate when one considers how many have assisted in such varied ways to make this book become a reality. I will try.

Special thanks must go to my beloved wife, Joyce, for her endless hours of editing, listening, traveling, balancing our belabored checkbook on my excursions to learn more about the subject of the Runestone as well as listening to my endless changes in wording and attempts to make this subject interesting and enjoyable to others. Her efforts on my writings may very well exceed my own.

Jeane Lewis (Emogene) Simpson has been more than merely an inspiration and encourager. I have given her the title of "Mom" and her love and strength has kept me plowing along for far more times than she would admit or probably knows. Her writings entertained and enchanted me over the decades as she read her handwritten manuscripts to a small, but enthralled, group of friends, to which I have the distinct honor of being included.

I greatly appreciate my three daughters' readings and input. What seems so crystal clear to me may be quite hazy to those that haven't read and reread the many books and documents I have while researching this book. Thank you for your love and the time spent helping me on this project.

Chet Noviki's books and encouraging remarks on bookbinding and other issues of publishing are deeply appreciated. He provided wonderful information that enabled me to do things that many others pay to have done. MA KIT PO AN, Amigo.

The Runestone Museum at Alexandria, Minnesota has been a wonderful source of information and seeing **THE ROCK** has provided me with a desire to help convince others to reconsider just who actually came to this continent first. Julie Blank, the museum's Executive Director, has been very encouraging and helpful.

The Heavener Stone in Oklahoma, which may predate the Kensington Stone by centuries, helped to convince me of the authenticity of these lonely indications and to prove to me that people of the North countries had been exploring here for centuries prior to Columbus.

Although I suspect that he'll never be aware of the impact his presence had upon me, a small, elderly, well-dressed man, with a white western hat and a huge smile on the Navajo (Ute?) Reservation in Arizona brought an image to me of what an ideal tribal leader should look like. Two characters of this book, Torowa and Nawha, are written with this very distinguished gentleman in mind.

The staff, officers and rangers at the Heavener Stone, Pipestone National Monument, Fort Abraham Lincoln, the Olof Ohman home, Fort Mandan, the Hjemkomst Center, the Swedish Institute, the Sons of Norway as well as numerous other sites and libraries have also contributed to this book by providing information useful in framing my thoughts.

I greatly appreciate Jim and Judy Servidio who have often concluded their remarks to me with, "Ralph, you should write a book."

Others in my corner include Alpha Engstrom, Bruce and Phyllis Anderson, Al and Lori Haapasaari, Vivian Sazama, and Shirley Schulz as well as those many friends that just keep telling me to "Write more stuff."

I tip my hat to you all in gratitude.

Ralph A. Mayer

Introduction

After having heard about the Kensington Runestone for many years and, with a large amount of the information being very skeptical, a visit to the museum housing the actual stone was not a top priority for me. Hearing it called a hoax by so many respected experts led me to think that Columbus' voyage in 1492 was probably the year of discovery of this land. This has now changed!

When it became an established fact that L'anse aux Meadows was indeed a Viking settlement on the northeast shores of Newfoundland a thousand years ago, I had to admit the possibility was enormous that the far-ranging and bold Scandinavians hadn't just squatted there but had wandered about searching for new places to trade, settle or - loot.

Even though the word 'Viking' is exceedingly popular in northern Minnesota, the men that came here would have used that word only to mean "pirate" and certainly would <u>not</u> have applied it to themselves. To call themselves "Vikings" would have probably been rude and insulting because the term "to go a-viking" referred to piracy and invasion of other peoples' lands. Just as they did <u>not</u> wear horned helmets, they were <u>not</u> pirates. Someone seemed to feel that the pictures of the ancient warriors looked more fearsome with horned helmets. They did not actually seem to have had such headgear. Sorry, Hagar.

The settlement in Newfoundland was given more solid dates of 900 to 1000 AD and that does fit well with the colonies in Iceland and Greenland of that early period. Columbus' voyage was not to occur for five more centuries and it was quite likely that the Scandinavians had done some checking into the possibilities of increasing their riches by getting more deeply involved in this new country. The Heavener Runestone found in Oklahoma may even predate the Kensington Runestone by several centuries in that the alphabet used on it is most often associated with the writings of 600-900 AD.

The 1354 Charter written for King Magnus indicates a reason for the Norsemen to enter this country other than just to become richer. They were seeking other Greenland colonists that may have been straying from the Catholic religion, which had replaced the pagan beliefs in Scandinavia. Copies of this actual charter are displayed in the Runestone Museum at Alexandria, Minnesota.

The Viking influence throughout Europe was substantial and could easily be traced from the Viking raiding trips to the more peaceful trading stations and ports they established throughout that continent. Could it be that the trips to the new world were just too long, dangerous and costly since they could get anything they needed much closer and more inexpensively? Atlantic crossings were notoriously dangerous and the loss of ships was very common.

The days of plundering had been replaced by trading and civilization had spread, as had a much less bloody religion. As Christians, dying in battle wasn't given the great rewards as in the past and thereby diminished the desire to race into deadly situations.

Any number of reasons may be argued as to why the Scandinavians did not settle here and thereby provide us with place names of more Norse and Viking heroes and less of the Italians who had arrived here five centuries later.

For decades, language experts argued that there were letters (runes) on the Kensington Runestone that were not in use during those actual years of the fourteenth century. With the passage of years and the discovery of ancient documents and stones, this argument has greatly weakened. Words that supposedly did not even exist in the language were said to have been carved on the Runestone, but now have been found to be legitimate and commonly used during that age. Wise people have disputed every possible angle of this stone and many have been called names in anger and slandered for having defended what they believe to be an actual ancient artifact. The Heavener Stone in Heavener, Oklahoma has runes carved into it that may date it to an even earlier expedition in that the runes are dated from the 600 to 900 AD. That particular stone had been known and commented upon by Indians as early as 1830, seventy years prior to Olof Ohman's discovery in Minnesota.

This book is being written to merely show how it may have been and I have endeavored to include as many actual facts as I could find. Since it is a historical fiction novel, my imagination has provided additional background to the story.

One has to consider what life was like at the time the stone was discovered and how the Ohman family suffered as a result of its presence on their land. The benefits for having discovered the stone were negligible and the shame and disgrace followed Olof to his grave. Even his children hated to even speak of it. Honest and hardworking more accurately described these early settlers rather than frauds or swindlers trying to make money for uncovering the rock.

I believe there were exploring Norsemen traveling about in this region six to seven hundred years ago. Considering the type of men they were, this feat, while difficult, would not have been impossible at all. In fact, it seems likely they were seeking places to mine minerals, trade, settle or just find errant Greenlanders that may have wandered into this country without a Catholic priest to serve them.

Evidence has been commented upon in numerous writings of blond, blue-eyed Mandan Indians having been seen in the eighteenth century. Holes bored in mooring stones along what had been waterways back then, fire starting steels, ceremonial battle-axes, swords as well as other very outdated artifacts found on farms in the vicinity of the Kensington Runestone have strongly reinforced my belief.

These proofs are all available for the interested visitor or scholar to observe in the Runestone Museum in Alexandria, Minnesota. The actual stone stands there silently holding the secrets as to its origin. Many thousand visitors from all over the world come annually to gaze upon the gray stone and consider its origin.

The arguments may continue for some time to come as to whether these men came here. For my part, I will respectfully quote Edward Ohman, the son of the man that discovered the Kensington Runestone, when he said, "Them boys was here alright!"

I think so too!

Ralph A. Mayer

Table of Contents

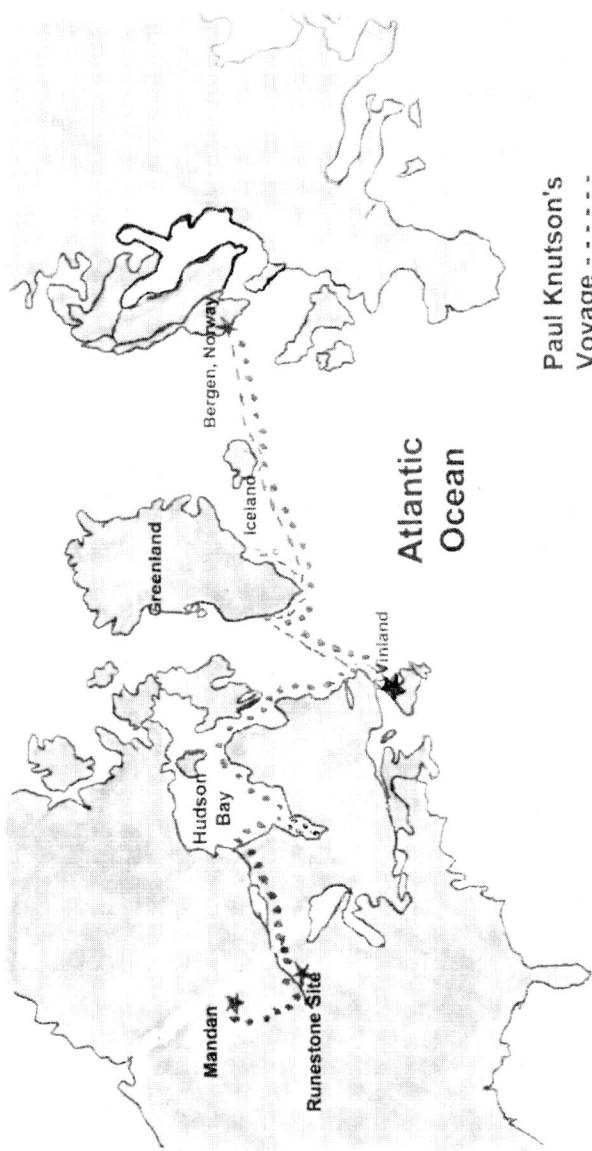

Atlantic Ocean

Greenland

Iceland

Bergen, Norway

Vinland

Hudson Bay

Mandan

Runestone Site

Paul Knutson's Voyage - - - - - - -

Bjoro Anderson's Voyage · · · · · · ·

CHAPTER ONE

Olof Ohman's Discovery

"Papa, come look at this!" said the boy to his father in Swedish, while rubbing his cap on a large piece of overturned rock.

Olof Ohman left his team of horses and approached his son. He looked with interest upon the large, flat, gray rock wrapped in the roots of a large aspen tree they were removing to clear a new field in preparation for tilling. The tree had been difficult to tip over and this explained why the horses had such a hard pull. The roots of the aspen, which had stood as a sentinel, were several inches thick and strong because the tree had probably been embracing the stone for twenty, thirty or even more years. Many of the thick roots were flattened, squeezing the stone, as they slowly grew around it.

Leaning upon his double bitted axe, Olof's first impression was that they had uncovered a tombstone as he could see there were markings of some type etched into it. Chopping away the roots and releasing the stone from the grip of the tree, Olof used a stick and leaves to wipe the damp soil from the face of the rock. The middle-aged farmer was momentarily concerned he was disturbing a grave.

Prior to the mid 1800's, there hadn't been many white men in this west-central part of Minnesota except for the French traders and other explorers who may have trekked through here and buried their dead as they traveled. The farmer studied the smooth face of the rock as he felt some concern about perhaps having someone's grave on his property. He recognized the markings on the stone as an unfamiliar form of writing but what it said was a mystery to him.

He'd seen headstones and crosses in the yards of nearby neighbors where their dead had been buried, as church or local cemeteries were not available to everyone in these parts of the sparsely inhabited frontier. Most of the grave markers were constructed of concrete, wooden crosses, a rock pile or simple slabs of wood. Carved granite was usually seen in cities and churchyards and most often only by the wealthy members of society.

1

Olof's ability to read was severely hampered by his lack of formal education. Times had been hard and he'd gotten the total of a few months education in his younger life. The majority of Olof's education was mainly a result of learning skills from workmen and other farmers.

Olof had been born in Sweden where the population was too heavy for a man to establish himself as a farmer unless he rented land from someone else and even that had become difficult. Olof's father liked the idea of having independence and the ability to farm his own land in the Americas. They had moved to the United States with high hopes, a desire to make a secure living and have the ability to take care of their own family.

After standing in the August sun for a few moments studying the stone, Olof questioned the writing upon it. He wondered if it indeed was a headstone for the dead. Even with his untrained eye, he could see it had been roughly scratched out and chiseled by hand. The stone had enough symbols resembling letters to make it obvious that someone had wanted to record a message they had felt to be extremely important.

Olof thought one should show respect for the dead and, if there was a grave here, he wondered if it would be proper to plow around it as he put in his crops. He hadn't been informed of a cemetery on this property when he purchased it and he felt it was an annoyance to have to plow around the rock. However, if it was the final resting place of someone, he felt he might have to consider it. It occurred to Olof there could be other stones in the vicinity indicating burials, but he hoped this was not the case. He needed that room for crops.

In the meantime, many other trees would be removed. He would find someone who knew about graves, headstones and that sort of thing. Olof was a farmer and some things just couldn't wait. He was eager to plant these newly broken fields and required the extra acres to feed his large and growing family

One of Olof's sons remarked, "We may have uncovered an 'Indian almanac', Papa!"

Since most of the neighbors had not been educated much beyond what he was, Olof felt that maybe a more educated person could come out and give an opinion as to what this two hundred pound rock was supposed to be.

Whatever it was, having been buried this long, he felt no one would ever get too excited about it. He thought maybe he could get

Sven Fogelblad over to take a look at the stone. Sven had been a minister back in Sweden and was well educated. Even though he had left the ministry years ago, he was a popular figure in the neighborhood and willingly assisted the neighbors with the interpretation of legal papers, complicated documents and questions that may have puzzled the common farmers.

Olof's closest neighbor, Nils Flaaten lived only a few hundred yards away. Nils had been on that farm for several years before the Ohmans had moved here. Olof thought about asking Nils if he might know what this heavy gray chunk of rock meant and if there was a cemetery here. Nils knew Olof was working on this grove of brush and trees and if there had been something to be concerned about, he'd surely have mentioned it. They were close friends and often had coffee together and visited.

This rock was already a nuisance, Olof thought. He could dump it on the stoneboat and drag it to the growing rock pile to be flopped amongst the other bothersome rocks that had been dug from the newly broken fields. But, being the rock was rectangular and flat, Olof also thought it could be put to use on his new farm somewhere.

Times were hard and everything had to be put to use. A nice flat rock could be useful in the yard as a place to straighten nails or staples and other farmyard tasks. If it weren't anything sacred or a headstone, maybe he'd use it for a nice step to the house or granary. It would be a fine place to stomp muddy boots upon or to tap out the remaining grain from the bottom of a damp bucket when feeding the chickens.

Olof considered these things and decided that the opinions of others may help the decision making process.

Eventually he came to regret his decision to inform others of this large gray mystery rock.

In the following weeks, the heavy rock had drawn a few curious neighbors over to gaze upon it and provide a variety of opinions. One of the Ohman boys used a nail to clean the carved letters (runes) to make the deciphering easier but the verdict was the same. It could be some form of language but the message was too ancient for anyone in the neighborhood to identify.

The Lutheran pastor from the Swedish church nearby couldn't read it but he came to the same conclusion as Sven as some markings

3

seemed similar to some ancient writings. At any rate, it didn't make sense to him and he mentioned that it was very likely "a pagan stone of some sort."

Even a Catholic priest from a nearby German settlement had made the trip over to look at the strange rock. His only remarks were that there were some odd marks he may have seen in some old books from the Cistercian order that had been in the library in his seminary. He thought, however, it was probably a coincidence as the Indians used many symbols that could be mistaken as those of the white men.

After a period of being displayed in a store window in the town of Kensington, Minnesota, the rock was to be studied and deciphered by a variety of scholars at the University of Minnesota in Minneapolis.

Olof was somewhat surprised to learn that the wise and educated men of the University had determined that the stone was a fraud and a hoax! What really bothered him was they were accusing him of being the perpetrator!

"I'm not even sure what language was scribbled on that rock much less having chipped it out myself!" Olof grumbled.

He felt insulted!

His neighbors knew he had not owned the farm at the time the tree started to grow over the rock. They were also aware the type of man Olof was and foolishness of that sort was not a pastime of his. Like all men of that time, he would enjoy a joke on someone else occasionally and laughed at some played on him but...this was different! His character was being challenged and he had no way of arguing his innocence.

Who hadn't had the lower side of a hammer handle smeared with cow manure and extended to him at a barn raising or a fat wad of straw packed into the toe of their overshoes? This was a manner of having a good time after an exhausting day of physical labor. The deep sounds of a bear behind the outhouse had caused many a young lady scampering, while pulling up their clothing, toward the house in terror with young men laughing themselves sick in bushes nearby having made those sounds themselves.

Olof had been involved in such pranks as a child and now limited his mischief to harmless fun with others that would bring immediate response. Even "dirty tricks" were known to occur at dances and get-togethers. "Dirty tricks" were tipping the outhouse onto its door with someone occupying it. That was the worst prank Olof could think of and he hadn't ever been a part of that one.

Pretending that the rock was real, if it wasn't, simply was not a part of his character.

Olof thought, "What would be funny about chipping a foreign language onto a stone that would not be seen for who knew how long? What a waste of time!"

The townspeople were the first to treat him differently. Rumors of him being the perpetrator of a hoax began trickling back to him from friends and neighbors. Most of the merchants knew him to be a totally honest and trustworthy fellow who would not be apt to involve himself in such a prank.

Olof had been known to display a nasty temper if the need arose but his large presence was usually enough to prevent anyone from insulting him to his face. He was a powerfully built man and not given to nonsense, so very few people were disrespectful to him -- in person.

The local schools picked up on the interesting situation. The teachers quoted the papers and also the educated men of the University that first hurled the cruel accusation at the Ohman family. The insults soon reached the younger members of the family and trips into town became too embarrassing for them. The children became reclusive rather than face the taunting and the giggles.

As the years passed, the Ohman family suffered their fate but continued to farm the land that Olof had so painstakingly cleared. Olof never did find any additional evidence of anyone having been on his land before him.

He was an example of Swedish stubbornness and perseverance and the land, that he'd strained to clear and plant, was his own to live on and defend. Leaving the area was not a subject that he discussed.

However, mooring stones, that had been used to tie up the sailing vessels of the Norsemen, dot what was once the river system to this day as an indication of the landing spots of the intrepid explorers.

Years after Olof Ohman discovered the Runestone, occasional fire starting tools, swords and halberds were found in numerous parts of the Midwest. Runes possibly dating back as early as 600 AD also stand in Heavener, Oklahoma.

None of this would have meant much to the Ohman family because they had suffered much embarrassment, sadness and humiliation since they discovered the Runestone.

Olof Ohman had made the total sum of five dollars from the rock now called the Kensington Runestone.

The discovery of the Kensington Runestone occurred in 1898.

CHAPTER TWO

The King's Charter

Magnus Ericksson, King of Norway, Sweden and Skaane, was seriously concerned about his eternal salvation. It was his responsibility to provide spiritual supervision for the countries under his jurisdiction as well as the colonies and there seemed to be an extremely serious situation in the settlements of the west.

It had been brought to his attention that some of his subjects may not have been receiving the proper spiritual direction and this problem was directly pointed back to the Crown.

The colony of Greenland had at one time seemed to be flourishing but the reports recently showed that the church may not be guiding its subjects properly and they were in need of leadership. Furthermore, the subjects appeared to have left the colony and were living somewhere else where the church could not reach them. It being the King's responsibility, he felt the salvation of these people could certainly affect his own personal salvation if he didn't enthusiastically respond to the need.

Those missing people needed to be found and given the proper teaching in the Catholic faith. The King was determined to do whatever was required and provide them with a priest or bishop to help remove whatever influences could be deceiving them. The pagan beliefs of their ancestors were not too deep in their past and some may have wished to cling to them.

The King perhaps wasn't aware of the heavy hand the church had placed upon those subjects living in the colonies. By using the powers and authority of their offices, the church leaders had sapped away the wealth of the people to the degree that the farmers became serfs on the property they had once owned and tilled. Everything went to the church and even more was demanded. Inheritance laws had cost them their homes to the church so when they had eventually suffered enough, the hardy Norsemen moved to other shores leaving the powerful church run government behind.

Other factors included the increasingly severe winters in

Greenland, causing loss of crops for them. The invading Skraelings (Eskimos were called by this title in Greenland but the same term applied to the Indians of the mainland) were becoming more of a nuisance as they too had severely suffered from the worsening cold weather during the past decades and they were not above invading the land of the invaders.

King Magnus found a trusted and seasoned sea captain by the name of Sir Paul Knutson and directed him to find the missing subjects of Greenland. He also assigned Nicholas of Lynn, a Franciscan Friar and astronomer to assist in navigating the vessel. The ship was a knorr type that could handle the North Sea if the crew did their jobs well and if the weather wasn't too bad. The loss of ships was far too common and, as a result, many lives of Norse seamen had been lost while battling the turbulent northern ocean.

The King drew up an official charter and Captain Knutson searched for a capable crew. The King had assigned four of his personal bodyguards to accompany the ship to assure that the King's orders were obeyed. These additional soldiers annoyed the captain, as every man on his ship was expected to do sailors' work to make the trip. His annoyance was further increased when the Friar Nicholas convinced the King to send a second priest to leave behind with the errant runaway subjects if and when they were found. That would be six inexperienced, idle hands aboard to cross the North Atlantic Ocean and Captain Knutson felt this was not the way to run a ship properly.

Captain Knutson knew they would be facing prevailing westerly winds on their outward-bound portion of the trip, which required solid men at the oars and soft skinned land men could cost them dearly. Returning home wouldn't be a Sabbath afternoon's rest either if any of the men were killed while facing dangerous situations. They could come up shorthanded!

The King did not appear to respect the North Sea enough to listen to good advice and they could pay dearly for that. Sir Paul Knutson had seen many well equipped ships lost, even with experienced crews and captains and he had hopes to return to his family and leave the life at sea for others after this trip.

Sir Paul was very well off financially and had been knighted so this would be his last North Sea crossing. King Magnus had personally requested Sir Paul direct this mission, as it was of extreme importance to the King that this voyage be a success and it was absolutely necessary for the King's eternal life.

Captain Knutson had enjoyed the last several months at home sitting with his beautiful wife, Margret, and enjoying the various wines that he'd been experimenting with for the past several years. He'd attempted to make wines from the many berries and fruits that he'd been growing on his farms and even made a considerable income from the selling of his delicious products. Sir Paul's beers were popular with the sailors and were now in continual demand in the nearby villages. An exporting market for his product had developed which had also increased his wealth.

During his trips to the countries south of them, he had watched the vintners and brewers make delightful drinks and had paid them well to teach him their secrets. Now he had become quite an expert at the winemaking profession.

Several of his crewmen had displayed interest and he'd assigned them to remain with the experts in those countries and study under them until they could also make wonderful alcoholic drinks of the various grains and fruits. He'd then hired them to work for him and he built homes for them nearby his own while his winery and brewery grew more successful.

Even King Magnus had ordered many large jars of Sir Paul's finest wines for his daughter's wedding and he proudly told visiting heads of state that the delicious beverage they were drinking was a product of his own kingdom of the north. Several of the local monasteries had made beers and wines but none could begin to compete with Sir Paul's.

As the knorr was being loaded prior to departure, the captain carefully placed a couple of well sealed, small clay jars of yeast in the tiny ship's hold, to allow him to make wines and beers as they traveled. Even potatoes and peas became delicious wines in Paul Knutson's hands.

Reports were that during earlier voyages, a land to the west of Greenland had been settled and was known as Vinland (now Newfoundland) due to the fine grapes growing there. This interested Sir Paul greatly! All of Europe would be eager to taste the drink from the wild lands across the sea. Thoughts of making an honest profit were never far from Sir Paul's mind.

In addition, the captain insured that the crewmember designated as cook was also well skilled in the brewing arts. A jovial monk had once remarked that the Holy Bible stated, "Wine cheereth the hearts of both men and gods". That obscure scripture became one of Sir Paul's most repeated as he toasted his guests and friends with a drink. Aboard ship, however, Sir Paul never permitted drunkenness, but every crewmember was given a pint of beer with the evening meal and a half pint of wine on Sabbaths while the supplies lasted.

King Magnus fretted about the success of this venture and provided the ship with equipment of the very best quality. He had an audience with the captain and friars just prior to casting off.

The King knew well the reputation of the treacherous North Sea storms. They had taken many a hearty ship and crew to the bottom and his fervent prayers were that this knorr be preserved to accomplish the serious task set before it. The document describing the task had been drawn up and signed and a blessing given to the voyage by the bishop as it prepared to depart.

This event occurred in the Year of Our Lord, 1354.

Magnus, by the grace of God, King of Norway, Sweden and Skaane send to all men who see or hear this letter good health and happiness in God.

We desire to make known to you (Paul Knutson) are to take the men who are to go in the Knorr (the royal trading vessel) whether they be named or not named, from my bodyguard and also from the retainers of other men whom you may wish to take on the voyage and that you (Paul Knutson) shall be the commandant upon the Knorr, shall have full authority to select the men who are best suited either as officers or men. We ask you to accept this, our command with a right good will for the cause inasmuch as we do it for the honor of God and for the sake of our soul and our predecessors who in Greenland established Christianity and have maintained it to this time, and we will not let it perish in our days. Know this for truth, that whoever defies this, our command, shall meet with our serious displeasure and thereupon receive full punishment."

"Executed at Bergen, Monday after Simon and Judah's Day in the six and thirtieth year of our reign (1354). By Orm Ostenson, our Lord High Constable, our regent sealed".

CHAPTER THREE

Iceland

Captain Knutson carefully chose the season and weather before casting off the lines from the homeland and beginning the journey to the west. He'd made the trip to Iceland a few times in the past but had never liked being in the North Sea with its fickle weather and icebergs.

Other skippers reported having seen the gigantic mountains of ice floating southward and the sight was reported to be awesome. Gigantic waves were known to slam ships into the walls of ice with a force of an egg hurled against a tree.

At least one crewmember was kept awake and alert at all times to watch and listen for these monsters should an abrupt course change be required at a moments notice. Dark and windy nights worried everyone as the wind could muffle the sounds of waves slapping at an iceberg until it was too late to avoid it.

As the master and the officer responsible, Sir Paul slept very poorly on such nights. An unusual noise would have the entire crew awakened and ready at their oars to make course corrections.

Sir Paul recalled the sagas of his Viking ancestors that had sailed these waters. Those seamen had sailed without knowledge of what may lie ahead and even with the concern that the edge of the earth may drop them into a pit of unknown horrors.

Even though Sir Paul was courageous and bold, he was glad he didn't live in the age of the Vikings when they had to forcibly wrest goods and property from their true owners. He far preferred bargaining and trading with no lives lost and a tidy profit assured in the future. Use of the word "Viking" was reserved for events dealing with piracy and Sir Paul would never consider being called a Viking. He felt some embarrassment while thinking of his pagan ancestors.

There had been instances when pirates and renegade groups occasionally attacked the Norse ships in the recent past. The thieves had wanted what the prosperous men of the northlands had and Sir Paul defended his ships and property with skills that had always sent the attackers running for their lives with furious and well armed Norse sailors killing any that were unfortunate enough to be caught. Pirates received no second chance to ever again attempt to annoy His Majesty's shipping.

The cold blood of their Viking ancestors still occasionally appeared when the need arose but this seemed to occur less frequently as the flags and sails of the Norse became familiar and welcomed throughout the continent.

Knutson's crews were superbly trained in the fighting arts and were willing to learn any new methods of defending their merchant ships. The tall, light skinned men of the north were now welcomed into ports and local businessmen eagerly made merchandise available for trade with them. Welcoming kisses, shoulder slaps and friendly greetings had long replaced the sounds of metal-to-metal combat. The need for Norsemen to 'go a-Viking' had been replaced with the solid and serious business of trading with anyone that had desirable goods to sell.

However, the men of the north were still in demand as bodyguards and mercenary soldiers to foreign governments largely due to their fierce ancestors' reputations. Many foreign rulers kept some tall, yellow bearded Norsemen as personal bodyguards as their fierce fighting reputation still followed them throughout the world.

As the small ship crept toward the island of Iceland to restock and prepare for the remainder of the trip toward Greenland and further west, Sir Paul recalled the stories of the captains that had previously been to Greenland. He remembered them stating that the settlements were found to be abandoned and appeared as though the former occupants had left in an orderly fashion. Villages, farms and churches were reported to be standing empty showing little indication of strife and no unusual number of graves or skeletons about the sites.

The captain and priests were instructed by His Majesty to carefully study and document all that they found when they arrived at the Greenland settlements before moving on.

The King had chosen well, as the assigned men were all known to be extremely bright and capable of discerning anything that could be considered unusual or out of place. Documentation was required for each site and the findings of this group would be studied and considered by the highest members of the court upon the ship's return to their homeland.

While stopping in Iceland to restock their supplies with fresh meat, vegetables and water, Sir Paul gave samples of his wines and beers to city and state leaders and assured them that the stock could be frequently replenished should they want more. He was quietly delighted to see the eyes of the recipients light up with pleasure after the first taste.

Before leaving for Greenland, he sent a plump package home to Margret with a sizable amount of money and requests for more of his product to be shipped to Iceland on the first available westbound ship. The king respected the traders' skills for increasing the country's treasury and encouraged them to make the most of every opportunity to do business.

Sir Paul's interest was piqued during conversations with the local leaders of Iceland as, when they learned of his destination, they commented enthusiastically about the incredible fishing off the Vinland coasts. He also learned there were trees in that region that could make majestic masts for their ships.

Iceland was more remote than the other parts of the kingdom and the people there were eager for any news coming from either direction. The Icelanders also possessed more knowledge of Greenland and Vinland (now known as L'anse aux Meadows on the northeast tip of Newfoundland, Canada) area than anyone else as they had received it firsthand from the shipmasters that had stopped there for repairs and supplies.

The traders of treeless Iceland were very impressed by the quantity and quality of the wood brought from the new lands and remarked how the spars and masts were of excellent quality. Combining the new lighter and stronger canvas sails with the powerful foreign masts allowed the ships to travel faster than ever before.

Sir Paul thought to himself that this information could be very profitable at the markets of Europe in the future. How many other marketable items might one find in that rarely visited part of the world? Could this be a marketing opportunity? This was a question that Sir Paul had frequently asked himself throughout his career and had made him a wealthy man.

Ships had been going to the lands west of Greenland for three hundred years or more and there were even settlements in the area of Vinland (northeast Newfoundland) that were well known. However, little communication had been transmitted over that period.

Those living there seemed to be satisfied with their lot and had little desire to return to the European countries. The sagas indicated that the bloody Viking urges of those living in Vinland had gotten them into serious trouble in Iceland and made them less than welcome back in their homeland.

Another saga occasionally heard in the seafaring circles mentioned a relative of Leif Erickson's by the name of Glom, who had sailed south on the eastern coast of the new land into warm seas and eventually sailing northward up a south flowing river to a fertile land many days into the mainland. His group had eventually established a settlement somewhere in the interior but all contact had been eventually lost with them hundreds of years earlier.

As Sir Paul's knorr was preparing to cast off from the coast of Iceland, several shopkeepers raced to the dock to give requests for the wines that had become the greatest news of the month. Sir Paul happily supplied them with his home address and a letter to Margret requesting her to get the delightful product sent as soon as possible.

Greenland was the next destination and Sir Paul and the two priests discussed what they would be looking for in that strange place.

CHAPTER FOUR

The Red-Haired Priest

The wind blew steadily from the west on the day of departure from Iceland as the knorr struck a course for Greenland. Sir Paul knew that the likelihood of getting a calmer day was small. He felt the task before them was uncertain at best and no more time should be wasted without risking running out of time before returning. Maximum speed would be required to avoid sailing in a North Sea winter.

To Sir Paul's great relief, the four soldiers of the King's Bodyguard were willing to take their turns at the oars so the ship had most of the passengers doing useful work. The soldiers knew the value of exercise and rowing kept their arms and shoulders in top condition.

The man designated as the second in command was Bjoro Anderson. He was a handsome man, in his mid-twenties, who bore the mantle of authority well. He was well muscled and totally capable of all sailing tasks as well as navigation, fighting, handling a crew of tough men and, most important in Sir Paul's eyes, wise trading.

Bjoro had previously sailed with Sir Paul on dozens of voyages and had been tested by having additional difficult tasks given to him by the ship's master. He had performed admirably on every occasion and could be trusted not only to carry out an order but, if the situation availed itself, to be innovative enough to improve situations.

"Dependable, trustworthy and a good Catholic. What more could I ask or expect," thought the seasoned captain. This was the highest praise Sir Paul gave any man.

While not having ever mentioned it to Bjoro, Sir Paul hoped that the time would soon occur when Bjoro would take over the traveling part of his affairs so that he could remain home with Margret and his winemaking business.

"Bjoro is ready to take his own command and I'd like him to be the master on a ship of mine," the captain continued in his thoughts.

The younger of the two priests had also noticed Bjoro and had been involved in many discussions with him during the voyage. The two men had been born only a few months apart. Father Pettersson had developed a considerable respect for the young man and marveled at how many subjects they could discuss since Bjoro had received little formal education. Even discussions on subjects of a religious nature had become stimulating as Bjoro asked questions that would have been expected from only theologians.

"What this man asks is more relevant than most of the foolishness we discussed in our classes in the abbey," the red-haired priest concluded.

One of their discussions had been about the subject of laughter. The priest, of the Cistercian order, had commented that he'd met a group of brothers in a Benedictine monastery that had condemned laughter as a tool of the devil. While his personal beliefs didn't agree with that, he decided to introduce the thought to Bjoro.

Bjoro thoughtfully remarked, "Isn't joy a fruit of the Holy Spirit so thereby making laughter a good way to display this joy?"

At this the priest smiled and went on to comment "We humans are the only ones of God's creatures to have the capability to laugh…or blush."

At that, Bjoro responded by saying, "Humans are the only creatures that have the need to blush but laughter shouldn't be repressed. It's a beautiful gift!"

"This man would have made a marvelous priest," decided the man in the black robe. The discussion continued for a few more moments and concluded with both men laughing heartily.

The red-haired priest's father was a counselor in the King's court and had been frequently sent to the courts of other countries to negotiate important issues for the King. His father, like the priest, was a small man, but one of the true intellectuals of his day becoming well known and widely welcomed in the intellectual circles of the day. He had particularly enjoyed a visit to Italy in which he was invited to address a group of scientists and doctors. He found they attentively took notes of every word from his mouth and begged for diagrams and formulas from him while he was obeying King Magnus' order to make friends with the royal circle. Requests for his return to Italy had reached the King's chambers for decades and other trips had been provided for the brilliant Norse nobleman and scholar.

It was on a mission to Ireland that the priest's father was visiting the Irish court when he'd met the beautiful red-haired daughter of an Irish nobleman. Totally smitten with her intelligence as well as striking beauty, he soon convinced her to become his wife.

She agreed, but only after emphatically stating that the only condition of the marriage was to have their first-born son come back to Ireland and become a priest in the Cistercian order.

At the age of twelve, their red-haired son returned to the land of his mother and grandfather to study to be a man of God in a Cistercian monastery.

While he'd studied well and was determined to be a good priest, the priesthood probably wouldn't have been his choice of vocations had he been allowed to choose his own. As a priest, he had access to the best of libraries and this allowed him to study subjects that were beyond the reach of ordinary people. His own father's extensive library had given him an enormous advantage as a student. Library privileges had always pleased him immensely.

His Bishop once remarked, "All that reading stunted his growth." Five and a half hours of sleep per night was as much as Father Pettersson seemed to require and his small frame was often seen slumped over a rough desk in the abbey's drafty rooms both late at night and early in the mornings.

As a priest, Father Pettersson learned and performed well and was respected as a devout man and could be trusted to do any job well. He'd been watched carefully as he learned the skills necessary to become a good Cistercian monk but his curiosity did concern those above him in rank. Everything interested this man and he had a desire to learn about everything that he saw. Science was a passion of this black robed man of God.

He asked questions to the point of being a nuisance to anyone that he considered wise enough to have answers. However, not everyone had the solutions to his problems and this made his presence occasionally uncomfortable for some.

He would even question some of the church's teachings, even though he was told to accept some things on faith. His answer was, "We are told, in Holy scripture, to prove all things" and that didn't always set too well.

Father Pettersson wasn't welcome in all church circles as a result of his questioning nature. However, his great knowledge of medicine and astronomy made him a welcome part of Sir Paul's Greenland expedition.

CHAPTER FIVE

Greenland

Upon arriving in Greenland, the Norsemen stared gravely at the remains of the once thriving Viking village there. Only the stone and concrete walls remained of the buildings, as all the wooden parts were totally gone. Long cold remains of Skraelings' campfires indicated the presence of invaders that had used the precious wood for cooking and warmth.

The Norsemen carefully walked over the entire area with an occasional stop to pick up some artifact or unusual item that gave them some evidence of what had occurred here in the past decade or two.

The largest building had been the church with its high walls and gaping windows, which stared back at the group of explorers. Since the Skraelings' presence had been noted, no building was entered or corner turned without the well-armed men carrying their unsheathed swords. The four soldiers of the King's Bodyguard were the first to enter the sanctuary.

Seeing it to be empty, they crossed themselves reverently and called the priests into the abandoned room. Nothing of value remained and the benches, alter and stairs, which had been made of wood, were missing. The group of priests, soldiers and crewmen all stood quietly looking at the wall that once overlooked the alter and pondered the word scratched into the surface. **"THIEVES."**

Wordlessly, the two priests looked at each other and the same thought crossed their minds. Skraelings would not have been the ones to leave that remark. There had obviously been trouble here between the villagers and the church.

The younger priest had immediately noted upon landing in Greenland that the homes and businesses were very modest in sharp contrast to the huge and, at one time, magnificent church building. He was well aware of church excesses in some areas of Europe and had even witnessed some instances of it, so this was very likely a situation where the population had been financially bled by the church to the point of rebellion.

He also knew that pagan beliefs were still quite common back in Norway and Sweden and the Catholic Church had been having difficulty making inroads in many communities for decades and even centuries. He wondered how the former citizens of this village had felt toward the clergy and how the bishops and priests had fared before the town became deserted.

If paganism had been accepted again, there would have been little reason to keep any representative of the Holy Faith. A shiver ran down his spine!

There was no tangible evidence of warfare having occurred in the immediate area of the village or even anywhere else within several miles of the village. While it couldn't be ruled out, it seemed that there would have been graves to count in those last days but the dates on the boards in the cemetery seemed to be in a normal order of natural deaths with no particular group being buried, as there would be in warfare.

He recognized one of the most recent burials as being that of a priest but there were several other graves following his death separated by several months each. Apparently, the clergyman wasn't the last to die here. This was only slightly reassuring.

Several more abandoned villages were inspected on the south and west shores of Greenland. The similarity between them all was obvious. The one thing that struck all the Norsemen as peculiar was since the weather was so cold and unpleasant here, why would anyone have ever considered coming here to live in the first place?

The Norsemen were dressed in their warmest clothing and some were wrapped in the canvas that was used for sleeping. This was the summer season so the climate surprised them with its fierceness.

Crops would be nearly impossible to grow, wood seemed almost nonexistent and any type of food was very scarce. The Norsemen could hardly find edible wild plants here to restock their ship adequately to go any further.

While they had not seen any Skraelings (Eskimos) to this date, the mere fact that enemies were present might have been enough to make the earlier settlers seek other shores and climates but that seemed unlikely. Bleak Iceland at least had the hot springs to enjoy compared to this God forsaken place that had foolishly been named Greenland.

The Norsemen were feeling more and more eager to leave this desolate Greenland coastline for their western destination.

While exploring the western banks of Greenland, Skraelings were seen to be observing the Norsemen while they were examining another abandoned village. When contact was attempted, the Skraelings rapidly disappeared and were seen running away far in the distance.

"Skraeling" was the term, often used with some amount of contempt, of any native people living in the colder regions or even the far western area of their exploration. It came to include the Eskimo as well as the Indians that the Norse encountered.

"If these are the enemy that frightened off our villagers, we must be related to the biggest cowards ever to have lived," remarked Bjoro to Captain Knutson.

Pausing for several moments, Sir Paul replied, "These natives may have made a considerable amount of mischief but they didn't frighten the villagers to the point of leaving. Norse people are not so distant from our Viking ancestors' blood to leave a coward's trail. No, Bjoro, there were other considerations here and we can only hope to ever hear a human explanation. Perhaps in Vinland we'll find answers to this problem."

The crew spent several days attempting to find greens enough to supplement their diets on board. The mosses and lichens growing on the sides of rocks and stone buildings were collected and carefully stored aboard the ship.

The younger priest had gained a considerable amount of knowledge of medicine and had read the books of many authorities written over the years. Europeans often tended to shun the precious knowledge written by other cultures and, as a result, health and diet was sorely lacking in most countries of Europe.

Superstition had prevented many fruits from being used to improve health and the cause of diseases was typically attributed to a variety of totally unrelated sources.

Father Pettersson had discovered many old Moorish documents pertaining to medicine and health in a Benedictine monastery and had accumulated enough knowledge of their language to interpret them.

He had written notes to study and give to other medical doctors. It was in these papers he learned the positive results that occurred by the use of cleanliness.

The "Black Death" was currently crisscrossing Europe and the dealers in cures and relief were myriad.

None worked!

The young priest, who had been named Conn Pettersson by his parents, but nicknamed "Father Carrots" behind his back by the crew of the knorr, was a student of all sciences. He was curious as to why the plagues didn't affect the Jewish population to the degree that it did to others.

He'd been assured, by his superiors, it was mainly due to dealings the Jews had with Satan that they were spared. The priest had noted, however, the Jewish population tended to be cleaner and had followed a healthier diet. They also had their own well-read physicians, which provided a strong argument against the satanic accusations. He compared the Moorish writings with the Jewish physicians techniques and found a common connecting link. Cleanliness!

The young priest further noted that rats and fleas seemed to be more common where the plague was the worst. Therefore, he strongly recommended that the crewmembers declare war on rats and fleas on board the knorr to reduce the risk.

While the crew felt him to be a bit extreme, they did obey and managed to sharply reduce the population of the deadly creatures on board. Everyone hated the creatures and didn't realize, until the priest told them, that their lives might be spared as a result of the act of tidying up the ship.

In Greenland, it had been considered that the plague may have wiped out the villagers but it became apparent this had not been the case as there were no skeletons or other evidence to prove it had traveled across the sea to Greenland.

The priest hoped their ship wasn't carrying the "Black Death" with them!

CHAPTER SIX

The Black Plague

The crewmen stood in astonishment at the glistening sea before them. The sea glittered due to the untold millions of cod swimming near the surface in these waters.

After a half hour of fishing, the hold was overflowing. The men were ready for some real food as the moss and lichens scraped from the stones of Greenland had merely partially filled their stomachs and slightly reduced the pangs of hunger. Moss didn't have the delightful sensation provided by actual food and this blessing was totally appreciated.

After they had their fill of the incredibly delicious fish, most of the crewmen sprawled on the deck of the knorr in contented sleep. It was the first time in several days they had received enough to eat. Sir Paul also provided them all with a generous portion of wine with this being the Sabbath.

The sails were propelling them nicely to the west and landfall in Vinland was expected in the next few days if nothing interfered.

Sleeping soundly, no one noticed the flea-infested rat moving amongst them, gnawing on the remaining pieces of fish that hadn't been thrown overboard and may have been saved by someone for the next snack.

While the rodent was slipping under the covers of the sleeping men, fleas were leaping to the clothing of the sleepers and attaching themselves to the new hosts.

It was only a few days later that a soldier of the King's Body Guard complained to Father Pettersson of swellings in his armpit and groin. Later that same day, another soldier complained of the same symptoms. The diagnosis was that they were indeed infected by the Black Plague. Fear and dread immediately filled the ship.

Everyone on the ship knew that these men would not see another week to its end before death overcame them. The plague had been running rampant in Europe for years and this ship had recently been to an Italian port before being commissioned for this trip and that place had been found to have the disease.

Stories of ships entering ports with most of the crew dying or dead were heard everywhere. Ships had been found run aground with all hands aboard dead from the plague. Priests and doctors had some of the shortest life spans as they were in the presence of death more than anyone. Jews, lepers and others were massacred after being blamed for the disease. Any group that didn't have huge losses to the death was often blamed and many innocent people were killed.

The handsome young giants of the King's Bodyguard were the first to show the deadly symptoms of the Black Death.

They had been sleeping closest to the hatch through which the rodent had escaped from the tiny lower deck. These men had been working in the King's palace and fewer rats were there to contaminate anyone. They may have had reduced immunity having never been exposed to the degree that the sailors and others were. Normally, citizens of the lower classes suffered the greatest losses.

The younger priest recognized the problem immediately and knew all too well the seriousness of the situation. Segregation of the infected was nearly impossible on the tiny ship but he knew the only chance of survival for any of them would be to prevent the spreading of the disease in any manner that he could. Since there was no space for quarters below deck, everyone had to stay in the only area available and that was on deck for twenty-four hours a day and at as much distance from the infected men as the small deck of the knorr allowed.

The search for the rat became a matter of life and death as all the contents of the hold were brought on deck and totally examined. The young priest then ordered two of the youngest and thinnest seamen to completely disrobe and go through the hold with sticks to strike the offending beast when it was seen.

The rodent was eventually found in a disgusting pile of shavings in the bow of the craft and killed. The priest then ordered that the nesting area and all debris, that could possibly harbor fleas, be scraped up and thrown overboard. The young men were then ordered to jump overboard and swim to assure that the fleas hadn't jumped on to them. He wanted them to then go back into the hold with a small brand of fire to scorch the infested area, but the chill of the ocean water had them both shaking too violently.

Stripping off his robes, the red-haired priest descended into the hold with a small burning brand and had several leather buckets of water carried down to prevent the ship from catching on fire. Bjoro, the first mate, assisted him by carrying some pieces of canvas to slap water unto the seared boards. The priest knew that fire would destroy the fleas' eggs if there were any here as that could be the cause of all their deaths.

Father Carrots tried to reach into every seam and touch each board below the decks with Bjoro following immediately behind to assure that no glowing spark remained to ignite their floating sanctuary.

The priest knew that the black rats were known for being heavily infested with fleas and had studied the disease to the point that he totally disagreed with the typical physician's opinion. His thirst for knowledge had placed him in the forefront of the leaders of science in his day. He could prove more superstitions to be incorrect than most leading scholars.

His intellectual father had been tutoring him in his first twelve years of life and taught him that he had to justify everything by proof and reason. This did get him into trouble on many occasions, as he would offer explanations and solid proof to his superiors only to be soundly scolded – and usually ignored.

It was this very trait that caused him to be sent away from the churches in Europe. A kindly bishop suggested that he enter the King's service after a furious red-faced senior priest demanded that he be defrocked for heresy.

With the rat killed and the ship cleansed as best it could be, the fearful crew could only observe the ailing soldiers. Within two days, the other two guardsmen were displaying symptoms and three sailors were ill.

The former Viking village in Vinland came into sight before noon and the captain ordered haste in landing there to treat the sick on shore.

Nothing remained there of the village other than collapsing walls and a few pits that had caved in since the inhabitants had died off or left. A shattered bowl and a clay bottle with a broken neck were the only evidence of anyone having been here in a hundred years. That alone did show, however, that someone, even if perhaps only a ship that had stopped here to restock, had occupied this place.

One of Father Carrot's most treasured possessions was a piece of rounded glass that magnified anything small that he wanted to study. Using the glass, he studied the broken bowl and, after a short time, looked up.

"This bowl appears to have been made by the same person as some of those broken vessels in the main village on Greenland," he commented. "The maker made a design that is unique enough to identify it. See the tiny scratching of a seagull on the bottom as well as the side? I found those on a few broken bowls back there in the main village. Someone had stopped here for at least a time."

"They didn't make any improvements on the place, it would appear," stated Sir Paul. "I wonder if they ever wanted to be found."

Remembering seeing the word "THIEVES" back on the wall of the Greenland church, none of the party wanted to respond.

Hunting parties sent out by Sir Paul provided game for the ship and fish were very plentiful. However, with the plague on board, the chances of the crew getting back to Norway alive had diminished considerably. Captain Knutson had hoped to find the missing villagers here but they had left very little evidence to consider.

Sir Paul had carried a rough leather map showing a long coastline going to the south and it also indicated that they might be on a large island here with an inland sea to the west.

Remarks written on the rudimentary map stated that Skraelings inhabited the southern shoreline, as well as the eastern rivers, and were unusually vicious. The inland sea had not been explored other than to sail into it and comments were made that whales played there and enormous moose grazed in the water. They were described as huge deer with flat horns.

The two men of the King's Bodyguard, who had displayed the first plague symptoms, died on the second day in the ancient village at Vinland, and the other two on the next day with one sailor also dying. Three other men were showing symptoms of the plague and were in various levels of the disease with death being certain in another day or two.

The young priest directed the nursing of these men and demanded as little physical contact between the afflicted and the healthy members of the crew as possible. He kept the infected men in a shelter that was merely three partial walls but they covered it with sticks for a roof and the ship's sail for protection.

The rest of the crew was to stay several hundred feet to the west of the sick men so that the wind would not be so apt to carry the disease toward them.

Sir Paul had some serious decisions to make in the next day or two that would affect the remainder of the trip and his crew.

CHAPTER SEVEN

The Second Trip

Captain Paul Knutson thought long and hard before announcing to the remaining crew that the voyage of exploration was over and they were going back to Norway. Nearly half of his crew had perished from the plague in the past three weeks and now there seemed to be a plague free period that allowed him to assess the situation and make that decision.

He didn't want to be at sea with the plague on board nor did he wish to take it to any place that was free of it. He wasn't sure just what the young priest knew about medicine or disease but the fact that the entire crew wasn't infected amazed him. He'd fully expected to die here in this strange land. It was only when he had allowed the young priest to direct the care of the dying men that he realized there were methods of treatment that had not been explored before.

The trip back to Norway went well as the westerly prevailing winds filled the sails and the hold contained several hundred dried codfish. Stops in Greenland and Iceland for fresh water and food were the only breaks in the eastward trip.

Both priests, and about half of the crewmembers as well as Sir Paul and Bjoro, had survived the plague ordeal. They were present when the King requested the Royal Court be informed as to what they had found on the trip.

The King was deeply disappointed to hear that the missing Greenlanders hadn't been located. He said, however, that another trip would be organized in an attempt to locate them as well as inspect the huge inland waters and explore for other possible useful marketable products. King Magnus had a mind for business and this new country did interest him - a lot.

The King then asked Sir Paul if he'd consider taking another ship to the Vinland island but he wasn't totally surprised as the older sailor begged off. The King was interested in Captain Knutson's suggestions, though, as to how to staff another trip. Bjoro was suggested as being the master and the younger priest as the church's representative. Both of them had received valuable experience on this last voyage that could likely prove to be very helpful on the upcoming trip to the new country.

Finances had to be considered, however, and there were numerous situations that seemed to continually reduce the treasury. Considering the circumstances, The King stated that it could be years before the expedition could sail again.

During this time, the plague continued to periodically reappear in various places throughout Europe, Africa and Asia and the death toll became enormous. Superstition had overtaken reason and few had any hopes of escaping this horror once it erupted in a region. Entire towns had totally died off during this dark period.

Bjoro's younger brother, Ivar, had spent most of his life living near a large fjord in which the seafaring ships docked and unloaded the exotic cargo from their trips about the entire known world. He was only seventeen but had been helping to unload and restock the merchant ships for several years already.

Ivar's reputation as a good worker as well as a handy fellow to have aboard a ship, had made him popular with other shipmasters. Job offers were becoming quite common as he sweated to haul merchandise back and forth on the swaying gangplanks.

Bjoro had taken a ship filled with Sir Paul Knutson's wine to ports along the Norwegian coast and even well into Sweden. Bjoro wasn't apt to return to his homeport for another month or so. Selling Sir Paul's wine and filling the ship with merchandise to take to other ports for resale at a handsome profit had given Bjoro a measure of wealth that pleased him and his parents. He sailed for Sir Paul and answered to him only.

Ivar had decided, if he were to go to sea, it would preferably be with his older brother.

Ander Ivarson, Ivar's father, had other plans for his youngest son. He'd been negotiating a marriage of Ivar to the daughter of a well-to-do merchant. Besides, having a son that remained on land and who didn't risk his life at sea, Ivar's father thought there would be an opportunity for his son to become a successful merchant under the guidance of his wealthy father-in-law. Of course, Ivar wasn't consulted on the matter, but that was the custom of the time and few disputed it.

The girl that was to be married to Ivar was not a young woman that had anyone courting her. Ever! She, her sisters, her mother and even her maternal grandmother all wore the same identical expression, which happened to be a severe scowl. In fact, the entire neighborhood referred to them as "The Scowlers". They rarely smiled for any reason and were, for the most part, quite unpleasant to everyone.

The thought of spending the rest of his life with that woman and the other women associated with her was not a pleasant prospect for Ivar. None of the "Scowlers" had ever spoken to him even though they attended the same church and they lived less than a mile apart from him.

Going to sea with Bjoro became more and more an acceptable alternative. Ivar was becoming uncomfortable with his father's choice of spouses and he thought there had to be something better for him. Avoiding the gazes of that group of women became an obsession with him. He knew they were sizing him up and discussing him at length, much to the enjoyment of his friends.

Bjoro's ship hadn't set all its lines at the dock before Ivar was on board and greeting his brother. He discussed the possibility of getting hired as a crewman and learning the trade of seaman from his well-respected brother. Bjoro knew about the plans their father had for Ivar and sympathized. He had known the "Scowlers" his entire life, too. Ander had also wanted Bjoro to marry one of the unmarried "Scowler" girls at one time. It was then Bjoro went to sea and remained unmarried.

Bjoro wanted to help his little brother out, but the ship had been doing well in making a good profit, and since the sailors were able to receive a portion of the profits, turnover of crew was slight. He simply didn't need any help, and his crew was an excellent one, so letting any man off wasn't wise. To replace a seasoned sailor for a seventeen-year-old stripling wasn't apt to benefit the ship.

Bjoro's family had been farming for centuries with an occasional seaman coming out of the family. Even these seamen often had farms and just went to sea during the months when tending the crops didn't make demands. This had dated back to the Viking days when invading and pillaging were a part of life. This seemed to work well with their pagan religion. Honest trading had not been an accepted way of life. Bjoro had heard the sagas of those days and felt that the recent changes had been an improvement in the lives of the Norse.

Bjoro hadn't been back at his home dock in Norway for a day before a message from Sir Paul arrived for him. Since Sir Paul owned the ship that Bjoro sailed, the request to come to the former captain's home wasn't unusual. In fact, Bjoro always enjoyed the hospitality of Sir Paul and Margret as they offered him their newest wines to evaluate with them, as well as to have a splendid supper and conversation. This request, however, was different than any prior visits.

The jovial winemaker welcomed Bjoro as he would have a returning son. It was a joy for him to entertain the man that brought in so much money as well as serving him so faithfully. It was obvious to everyone that Sir Paul was treating Bjoro in a fashion that indicated some special feelings for the younger captain. The reason for the visit, however, was more than the typical discussion of the latest trip.

"King Magnus spoke to me this past month, Bjoro," said the owner of the ship. "He is looking for a suitable ship and crew to return to Vinland and explore those inland waters that we would have traveled if the "Black Death" had not changed our plans."

Sir Paul continued, "The King knows I want to stay here and leave the sea to younger and stronger captains and we discussed several options that could work. He will provide a new, sea worthy ship that would move faster than my merchantmen and will finance another trip to find those Greenlanders that probably have gone pagan.

"He asked my advice as to who would be a superior master of the craft and be faithful in carrying out his request. Your name was the first to come out of my mouth even though you have made me considerably wealthier since you've done my trading.

"Bjoro, my son, would you consider going back to the new world to carry out the King's wishes?" asked the older man solemnly. "You've proven yourself at sea repeatedly and have been across once. Your chance of getting the information back to the King is better than anyone else that I could name. He asked me to help him with all the matters applying to the journey and I want to get the best captain I can find. That, my son, is you! Can I tell King Magnus that you'll serve for another trip?"

Bjoro didn't hesitate for more than a second or two before responding, "Yes, Sir Paul. Please inform His Majesty that I would be deeply honored to serve him again."

CHAPTER EIGHT

The Crew

Sir Paul suggested that Bjoro move rapidly in making a crew ready to leave as soon as a ship had been built and outfitted. To Bjoro's delight, the younger priest who had accompanied them on the first trip was sought to accompany them again and the King would once more provide four of his personal guards to see that his exact wishes would be carried out.

The red-haired priest, Father Pettersson, had been teaching in a monastery in Gotland when he was summoned to Norway to see that the King's strict orders would be carried out in the loading of the ship's hold as well as to assist as navigator and doctor.

Father Pettersson made it a priority to be sure each piece of equipment and every parcel of food for the new vessel were thoroughly examined before stocking it aboard. He fashioned rat guards on the lines attaching the ship to shore. The gangplank was used only during daylight hours as well as guarded at all times to prevent any rodent from crossing into the vessel.

The young priest had been ready to leave the monastery as the senior priests and brothers were troubled by his irritating questions and persistent need of proofs for arguments. The Bishop had heard about him causing the students to develop attitudes that demanded answers rather than to blindly accept every concept. Having the young priest leave on what could be a one-way trip allowed many of the church leaders to breath a sigh of relief.

It deeply saddened the younger priest, however, to leave the extensive libraries even though many of the most informative books had been destroyed and parts of the libraries were off limits to everyone. He'd always been fascinated by the new world and was eager to return, even though he would be the priest/overseer to remain with any Norse settlers found to be living there.

The younger priest felt he was a man under authority and would follow the official orders the Pope himself had cleared.

The older priest, Nickolas of Lynn, who had been on the first trip, convinced the King that only one priest would be required with probably so few, if any, of the Greenland Norse left. Nickolas also recommended the younger priest, Father Pettersson, take the trip because he thought the possible damage done by the young radical and his unorthodox ideas would be minimal with the escaped pagans

Bjoro was seeking a totally new crew, as he didn't want to reduce the effectiveness of Sir Paul's ships by taking away the men he knew to be good seamen.

His brother, Ivar, needed to get out to sea in order to prevent a sad marriage, so Bjoro quietly added his name to the crew list. A number of good men chose not to be included in the ship's company because trips like this were often never heard from again. The age of exploration seemed to be over and the European coastal sailing was far preferable to facing the wild North Sea.

Single men with no attachments were the type Bjoro sought and – he knew there were some who had other reasons to take a long voyage.

A young Finnish man appeared on the dock asking to be accepted for the trip. Bjoro didn't know the fellow but agreed to talk with him before an agreement to sail would be made.

King Magnus had recently attempted an invasion of the area later known as Finland, but quickly backed out when the Black Death viciously flared up there. That could have been a reason for the young man to leave but it seemed to Bjoro that the Finn spoke Norse too well for a typical Finn. It was several weeks later that the Finn's story came out, as told by one of the other sailors who had known him from a nearby village.

The Finn had come to Norway several years earlier to be a farm worker and was living with a local farmer's family. The farmer had a stout daughter who had become smitten with the tall, muscular stranger and had lured him into a nearby flax field for a little romance. While they were hidden by the flax, her father realized what was going on out there and, taking up a pitchfork, raced into the field to tell the Finn that he was about to become his new son-in-law and would no longer receive wages.

Leaving Norway and a forced marriage seemed to be very logical to the Finn at this point. He had eagerly listened to news of a ship leaving for the newly found land in the western sea and he saw a possible way out of his dilemma!

Bjoro studied the muscular arms, calloused hands and expressionless face of the Finn and decided that he probably knew how to work and could prove to be an asset on the trip. Eino Torro was hired as a junior member of the ship's company. Since his facial expression never changed, regardless of the situation, he soon became known throughout the ship as "The Mask."

A few younger men were also chosen for the trip to do the less desirable chores, as Bjoro knew their energy would be very useful.

A member of the King's Bodyguard suggested to Bjoro another possible addition to the crew. The man had never been a member of the Bodyguard but was greatly known in the military circles due to his incredible size, strength and warfare techniques. The man was a berserkr and stories of his methods of fighting were becoming sagas that groups of wide-eyed listeners listened to over and over.

A berserkr could fight to the last breath and would totally lose all respect of the enemies' weapons with only the total destruction of the foe as an end result. Such men were exceedingly rare and sagas of such men had been repeated in the camps of the Vikings for centuries. The berserkr's bravery was such as to charge to his own certain death unless the enemy could see him coming and escape. This was the typical scenario with a charging berserkr.

This man, of whom the guards spoke, was a giant in a land of many big men. He was probably the tallest man in the kingdom and his weight was over half again that of the typical King's Bodyguard, which was made up of many very large men. His courage was such that when he became enraged, he was virtually unstoppable. Even with arrows sticking out of his body, this insane warrior had been seen to slice a man in half with a specially made sword and axe. Such an event usually caused the battle to be terminated and a hasty retreat of even the bravest enemies rapidly followed.

What made the man even more unusual was that he had a mental age of about six years. His favorite pastime was playing with tiny children or small animals. He'd never been seen to hurt any small creature and would cry for hours at the death of a kitten. He only fought at the command of a few men whom he knew to be his friends and then would have willingly fought to the death. Just his appearance was usually enough to send soldiers scampering back in ranks to avoid a confrontation with this legend.

His name was Kare, and having been abandoned at birth, used no other family name. His unmarried mother died in childbirth and he was reared by a group of nuns in a convent until he reached puberty and was then sent to work for a living with whoever could use the help. An army officer had eventually allowed the huge, young, retarded man to accompany him so that the digging of graves, toilets, hauling wood and other simple but heavy chores could be done by a low cost servant.

In a skirmish in which his officer had been severely wounded, Kare was dragging the injured man back from the field of fighting. An enemy soldier was attempting to strike the fallen officer when Kare stepped in and, with his officer's sword, beheaded the enemy with what appeared to be no more than a gentle swat with the heavy weapon. His future was decided with this one act of mercy to his master.

Armor was immediately fashioned for the giant and the blacksmiths and armorers provided him with a huge sword and axe. Vicious weapons of war replaced his digging and chopping tools and his fighting training began in earnest.

His gentle nature was not accepting of the cruel manner of fighting that he was being trained to do. Somehow, the master had been able to have Kare shut out all of his sweetness and kindness and replace that with a total disregard for his own life and limb. A superman had been created and sagas were being refreshed with the latest exploits of Kare, the Giant.

Kare was considered for the crew on the voyage to the new world for several reasons. His incredible strength allowed him to handle two oars, as one was usually enough for a typical oarsman. Special length oars were provided with a seat amid ship just for him. With Skraelings being a chief concern in the new world, such an example of the Norse strength would get the attention of the red men and thereby perhaps insure the success of the mission. A plan to build smaller boats to get through rapids and falls was in place. Brute strength was needed to haul the heavy vessels over rocks and cliffs and Kare certainly would provide that.

The Black Death was still raging and invasions of other lands were postponed in Europe until that threat was reduced.   The Army languished for a time and – being Kare had an enormous appetite, he'd caused many a camp cook to complain.

Bjoro hoped the easily netted cod of the new world would keep Kare's appetite satisfied but he also knew that may be a task in itself.

Kare, the soldier, was now Kare, the sailor.

CHAPTER NINE

Departure

Bjoro and the red-haired priest/navigator, Father Pettersson, looked approvingly upon the newly built ship. They agreed it was well built for the North Sea crossing and would also serve well on smaller waters and rivers too.

They sailed it around the harbor and well into the sea to get the feel of the new vessel. They intentionally sailed into squalls with it to get the feel of rough water and were satisfied with the performance and handling. The two men had become firm friends on the last crossing and felt quite comfortable together in every situation. A smaller boat was to be towed behind for the inland rivers of the unexplored continent.

"Bjoro, have you any regrets about leaving home to seek our future in the unknown?" asked the priest of the captain.

"No, not really," responded Bjoro. "This journey has been on my mind ever since we returned from the last crossing. I'd like to see more of that land and perhaps find a way to transport goods back to Iceland or Europe. It would appear that there are trees for lumber that could be harvested and returned here if it could be done at a profit. There are also animal skins, strange plants that may be used as food, perhaps minerals and ideas of the Skraelings that could improve life here. We have seen the miles of codfish awaiting our nets. Who knows? With your curiosity, you may find things that we have never considered before. You are a curious priest, Father. I've never seen anyone with such an inquisitive mind."

"Yes, and believe me, it has gotten me into an abundance of trouble, too," answered Father Pettersson, chuckling. "There are an influential number of people who believe that we already have all the knowledge we'll ever need. There are those who burn books and destroy knowledge due to superstition and fear of the unknown. Many Moorish and Asian books have been destroyed because the authors are heathen but, the knowledge could help all men."

Bjoro smiled and nodded. "You are not of that group, are you? I've seen you crawling around looking at insects, the contents of a fish's stomach and tree bark with that little glass of yours that makes everything look large. I even saw you staring at snowflakes and the tips of a man's fingers with that device. Your curiosity may have caused some to ridicule you but I know you will find many useful things with your glass that we can't even imagine using only our eyes. There's a need for more curious people like you in this world!"

They silently returned their concentration to the ship as the deckhands were rapidly stowing cargo, painting, sanding off rough spots that could be troublesome on long voyages, as well as the myriad of other jobs that required completion before departure.

Between his trips to the new world, Bjoro recalled a recent visit to a sailors' inn at the waterfront near Bergen.

The decorations that hung on the wall were brought back by the grog shop's owner. He was a former sailor that had once, several years back, landed on a southerly shore of this new unknown country and immediately been attacked by Skraelings.

A lucky shot by one of the ship's archers killed one of the attackers attempting to climb aboard and this sailor had taken some of the weapons and garments of the fallen enemy when the attack was repulsed.

These keepsakes were of great interest to the sailors visiting the inn, especially those with thoughts of going to the far-off place themselves, and many discussions resulted from them. The arrows were studied, handled and checked over by the guests of the grog shop but the object that caused the most interest were the leggings of the fallen skraeling.

The bold enemy had taken scalps of his fallen foe and now wore them on his leggings as he charged the Norsemen that had landed on the shoreline of the Skraelings' lands.

There were three scalps on one legging and four on the other. Most of them were black, as was the hair of all Skraelings but - two were blond.

Invaders from the north had been here before and some had died at the hands of natives that didn't accept anyone on lands that they lived and hunted upon.

All of the many ships' crews in the seaport shared stories and many trips had been organized by the information learned by seafarer's conversations in shops such as this.

Bjoro looked at the blond scalps and then around the room. Every man in the room was light skinned and had light colored hair.

He had a strange feeling that the first owners of the scalps and he may have something in common. Many Norse sailors had made that trip and many never returned.

The sailor that had returned with the gruesome souvenirs had still another story to tell. As Bjoro sat listening to the aging seaman, he watched amazed as the man pulled a small clay bowl, with a hollow stem on the side of it, from a wooden box. The seaman then stuffed some strange herbs into the bowl of the pipe and got a burning ember from the cooking fire and ignited the herbs. Several puffs of peculiar smelling smoke came from the man's lips and nostrils.

Smiling, the man passed the pipe to the other men in the room and encouraged them to each take a puff. Laughing as each man coughed with the odd tasting smoke, the older sailor explained that this plant he was burning was found growing wild in the strange land far to the southeast. There was a Welsh settlement that had been living near the coast of that strange land for a few years and they had welcomed the Norse ships to their tiny colony.

The elderly sailor became solemn as he commented that the Welsh group had all seemed to catch a disease from the Skraelings and most of the colony had died from a "bloody cough". The Welsh willingly offered whatever knowledge they had of the country but they also suggested it was unhealthy for white men to stay in this place. It seemed that the air didn't agree with them and their lungs became weak and death was apt to be soon for all of them.

They felt the plant they smoked had medicinal qualities and had even given the sailors bags of seeds to bring back to their home countries. They showed the visiting sailors how to make the smoking pipes from clay and wood and praised the natives that had shown them this aromatic plant.

Bjoro wasn't impressed and quietly decided he had inhaled enough smoke from cooking fires to satisfy his body's needs for smoke. However, others seemed to be more interested in smoking the tiny bowl and one man even stated that he liked the taste of the weed as he chewed it. Many men wanted to continue passing the bowl around the ale room.

The tobacco planting experiment didn't flourish in the colder northern climates but a few plants were maintained for quite some time, providing the owners with an addiction that they felt was a blessing to their health.

It occurred to Bjoro that this plant might be grown in some of the warmer climates and sold in the north after ripening. This could even eventually become a rather modest business if enough people began to like it. Then he reconsidered.

"Who could enjoy this choking weed enough to want to buy it? But then again, some men seemed to enjoy smoking the pipe and it may truly be healthy, as the owner claimed." Bjoro thought as he dismissed the memory from his mind.

Farewells had been said to their families the day before and the crew prepared to sail on the tide of the next day. Having cast off all lines and using oars to make the turns in the crowded harbor, the knorr pointed her bow to the unknown west before hoisting the sails and the King's second voyage to the new world had begun. There were no wives of the sailors on the dock as none of the men were married!

Sir Paul had donated several cases of his wine for the sailors to use or to sell in Iceland. They opted to drink it and savored it greatly each day just prior to setting the evening watch.

Sir Paul had deeply influenced this venture. His discussions with the King had provided the voyage with a state-of-the-art ship, the most advanced weapons, new clothing, good food and a handpicked crew. His teachings to Bjoro were continually being used and his morality and leadership had always been the best of examples.

The first portion of their journey to Iceland went very smoothly without problems of any kind. The crew stopped in Iceland to replenish their stores and water and continued on toward Greenland.

The knorr was approaching the waters surrounding Greenland when the crew became aware of a heavy fog, which prevented them from seeing even a few feet beyond the bow. As there was no wind, oars were being used and the soft scraping sounds and the occasional grunts of the oarsmen were the only sounds to be heard. Voices were used with only the softest tones as every ear was focused upon attempting to hear the sound of water slapping the side of a mountainous iceberg, should they be approaching one. They had seen some of the floating giants in the past days and it greatly concerned them. Just scraping one could be a disaster and repairs at sea were difficult or impossible under the best of conditions.

Captain Bjoro had just moved to the very point of the bow and was concentrating on the sea sounds when he picked up a whisper of sound that differed from that of the sea sliding under their ship. He immediately gave the command to ship the oars and allow their craft to come to a standstill. In these northern waters, the sun had probably been up for hours already but virtually none of it filtered down to them through the intensely thick fog.

A rudimentary compass, made by a dangling magnet, kept them running in a westerly direction but no other navigation equipment was useful in such weather.

By now all hands were searching the wall of fog for a clue to the new sound. Cautiously, Bjoro yelled out a sound to see if an echo could be detected. The hairs on the back of everyone's neck tingled as the echo came back clearly from a short distance.

"Oarsmen, prepare to fend off icebergs," commanded the captain. This was a command that he'd never given before and it sounded peculiar to him as well as his crew. Their proximity to the iceberg was very close and it could have been on either side or in front of them. The command to reverse the rowing was given and the ship was reversed for several minutes as Bjoro kept the yelling up until it seemed that the return echo was somewhat further away.

A ninety-degree port turn was accomplished and Bjoro asked another crewman to come to the bow and yell out the sound that may have saved their ship from disaster. The sounds now seemed to indicate that the berg was behind and to their starboard.

When the sun finally broke through, the crew was in awe at the mountain of ice they had so barely missed. It was more massive than any building most of them had ever seen and they knew that only a tiny portion of it was visible. Even at a mile away, Bjoro suspected there was a huge amount of the same berg under them as they sailed past it with frequent glimpses back over their shoulders at the mammoth pile of ice.

Many more icebergs were seen as they moved westward toward Greenland. When they arrived in Greenland, they decided to rest for a short time before continuing onward toward Vinland.

Following a short stay and refilling their water barrels, they continued on toward the western new world.

As they journeyed on toward Vinland, Bjoro found parchment and seawater to be incompatible so he decided to use leathers made from animal skins to make his navigational notes and maps upon. Maps made on paper or parchment hadn't stood up to the tests given them by the sea and they had to be copied and recopied.

As Bjoro studied a map copied from one on to a wooden board he noticed it indicated two major water highways leading to the west from Vinland. The lower, or southernmost, waterway was a river that seemed to be filled with falls and rapids while the northerly route entered a huge inland sea occupied by whales.

Bjoro felt the northern route would allow them to enter the interior of the new land faster and also would have been a more likely route for the Greenlanders to use. He decided that would the best route to take once they departed Vinland. The unfriendly Skraelings (Indians) were said to occupy the banks of the river as they reportedly also did on the eastern shores of this entire land. These natives were said to be far more vicious than those of Greenland.

As they drew closer to the ancient camp on the Vinland shores of the new world (Lan's Aux Meadows, Newfoundland) where they'd buried several of their last crew, gigantic mountains of ice continued to be seen floating past.

When they arrived in Vinland, the priest, Father Pettersson, now called 'Father Carrots' due to his brilliant red hair, celebrated their safe arrival with a church service, giving thanks for a safe crossing.

The crew was delighted to find an unexpected patch of dandelions in an overgrown garden that had been planted by the past inhabitants of Vinland. They brewed a healthy refreshing tea before leaving on the route that would lead them to the southern shores of the inland sea. Clumps of dandelion roots were carefully uprooted and placed in a leather pail for transplanting at other sites. These dandelions would supply them with a constant source of medicine and tea.

Even though they had brought dandelion seeds in their ship for planting in the new land, they felt they couldn't have too much of a good thing. Every part of the precious plant had uses in healing a large number of diseases and the Norsemen happily drank the tea and ate the greens knowing that it was considered a miracle plant.

Among the tools that had been determined to be extremely important to take along on their journey were some heavy hammers and chisels, which they planned to use to bore holes in large rocks.

On previous journeys, the Norsemen had learned that tying down their ships to trees or other types of on shore anchoring had proved to be dangerous and even fatal unless they could make rapid retreats from the arrow firing Skraelings. They realized the untying of a knot could cost the crew some men before the craft could hastily depart. Something more efficient had to be used and they found mooring stones worked splendidly.

By boring a sizable hole of something about a thumb's breadth into a boulder that weighed as much as ten men or more, a metal pin could be inserted deeply into the rock with lines attached to it from the ship. Should a rapid departure be needed, simply pulling the entire pin would free them to leave at a moments notice.

As they traveled, every good campsite had the sounds of the younger men of the crew tapping out holes in the great stones for both current usage as well as the possibility of future use. This precaution may have saved their lives on more than one occasion.

On sites where the camping was exceptional, a small amount of white cement mixture, which had been carried with them, was used to create a circle that was added to the mooring stone. This was meant to attract their attention or that of other travelers. This cement was considered to have a long life and to be nearly indestructible. Having been used as ballast in the lower hull, it was replaced by rocks for the remainder of the trip.

CHAPTER TEN

The Runestone

The river craft had been sailing all day and Bjoro, the captain, told the crew it was time to moor the small boat and set up a camp for the night.

They found a lake with a flat shoreline that would enable the Norsemen to keep their shelters very near the boat in case of an emergency. They found Skraelings were always nearby and most had seemed to be very unfriendly, so a rapid departure was always considered.

The smaller boat had separated from the knorr two weeks before and sailed south on this great river from the inland sea (Hudson Bay) that had whales in it. Twenty men went with the crew that took the smaller craft and the other ten remained with the knorr at the mouth of the river on the great inland sea to wait for their return. The smaller and lighter craft had been towed from Norway and was now in use on the inland waters that would otherwise have been inaccessible with the larger ship. The crew of ten remaining with the knorr would have just enough men to take her back to Norway using the helpful westerly winds. The crew of twenty leaving on the smaller craft included three of the King's Body Guard, Bjoro the captain, Father Pettersson, Ivar (Shorthorn), Kare and the 'Mask'.

Falls and rapids gave the crew difficult challenges to cross and required all hands to lift, slide, drag or use any other means to get the smaller craft on the portion of the river where they could move in the water. The Norsemen realized they were more vulnerable to attack by the Skraelings during the portages than they were at any time on land. Therefore, they tried to use any method they could come up with to keep the boat prepared for a hasty escape to deeper water and to also distance themselves from the vicious Skraelings as quickly as possible.

As they traveled, the Norsemen continued to bore holes in large stones because they expected to be able to use them repeatedly in their return travels as well.

"This particular place should be used frequently," thought Bjoro, as they pulled into an area along the shore. "Good fishing, deer drinking from the river to hunt, nice camping spot and no apparent immediate threat of Skraelings."

Bjoro told his brother, Ivar, nicknamed 'Shorthorn', "Make a rock with an obvious design that can be easily seen from out on the lake."

Shorthorn bored out the hole in the rock and then drew a large circle on the mooring hole with a smaller one inside the first. Using the heavy hammer and chisel that every ship had aboard and treasured, he chipped the circles out in the brittle stone. When the circles were deep enough to hold the substance, he smeared a white cement mixture into them. The white ringed rock could now be seen from a considerable distance out in the lake.

As the crew settled in for the evening, the subject of farming this land came up. Everyone agreed it was far better land than what they had seen in Greenland or even at the abandoned village in Vinland. With land like this, why did anyone want to go to those cold, unpleasant places? They had been traveling in this land for weeks without seeing a single white person even though a Norse village had been established in Vinland three hundred years earlier.

A saga of a Viking named Glom entering this new land from a river that ran south had circulated amongst the seafarers for centuries and the Norsemen now considered the thought that the missing Greenland colonists may have gone in that direction. From what the Norsemen had seen of Greenland, going to the warmer southern lands would be a reasonable choice and would certainly make good sense. However, that would have meant sailing down the eastern coast and most previous attempts had often met with disaster and few had returned. Glom's travels would have predated the conversion to Catholicism by at least two hundred years and possibly more.

Since nearly all the crew had lived on farms at some point in their lives, they knew the value of good soil. They sifted the black, moist earth between their fingers and commented about how most of their countrymen would be delighted to have such fertile earth and that this land would be a wonderful place to live. It had enormous forests for wood to build with and use for heat, rivers to run mills and travel upon, good warm seasons and water everywhere - for drinking and for fishing. Many aspects of it reminded them of their homeland...only better. Much better!

Shorthorn was sprawled on the shore near the boat as the sun was setting.

"This is a very pleasant place," he mused. "Maybe someday there will be a village nearby in which every one will speak Norse and cows, sheep and horses will graze right here and drink from this lake." That brought a laugh from the crew.

The Mask responded by saying, "That will never happen. This land is far too enormous and no civilized person would come here except to explore it and now we've done that."

Flipping a small pebble off Shorthorn's chest, he continued by saying, "When you get a lot older and wiser, as I am, you'll know that a country such as this will always belong to the Skraelings and we'll remain across the sea." This remark brought another soft laugh from the sleepy crew.

The next day, a crewman found shards of pottery that may have been of the type made by the Greenland Norsemen. Using his precious magnifying glass, the priest studied each part of the clay dish for nearly an hour. He was especially searching for the tiny seagull symbol that he'd seen in Greenland and Vinland, but some pieces were missing and the maker's mark could have been on any one of them. No definite proof of the Greenlanders ever having been here was found and the search continued closely in the area where the find had been made. Skraeling pottery had been found too.

Since there hadn't been any cultivated fields or familiar buildings seen, the trail was elusive and perhaps non-existent. But the King, however, had insisted that they exhaust the search and, if Greenlanders were there, the Norsemen were instructed to find them and provide them with a priest.

This campsite was particularly suitable and appeared to be at a fine location. They could easily travel into other nearby regions while using this beach as a base camp. Bjoro decided they would plan to settle in for a possible stay of several weeks at this site. Many lakes were very close and any one of them could perhaps have a Norse settlement nearby.

Bjoro split his force into two groups and left ten men in the camp where the pottery pieces were found to continue the search there. He then took a group of ten other men on the boat to fish as well as explore the neighboring lakes and possible places that the errant Greenlanders could have settled.

Three of the King's Bodyguard had left the knorr on the inland sea to the north and came with Bjoro's exploring group. Today, one Guard remained with the group in the camp and the other two came with Bjoro on the exploring team. The priest, Ivar, the Mask and Kare also came with the party that left the camp.

No indications of Skraelings had been seen for days and the base was considered to be a safe area. The remaining crew, therefore, felt secure there and did not deeply concern themselves about an enemy attack.

As the men went about settling the camp and searching through the pottery pieces, they were totally unaware of the hostile eyes observing them from the nearby forest. The smoke of the first evenings' fire had been noted from across the lake and by morning, the site was being observed by over a hundred warriors.

The Skraeling warriors discussed at length as to what would be the best method of attacking the Norsemen. The beach area was a part of a clearing that would expose the attackers during the rush toward the invaders. Skraelings found hand-to-hand combat to be undesirable and costly in lives. Arrows were the first choice of battle weapons because shooting from the forest was too long a distance for accuracy.

Seeing the Norse party split up meant that a loss of life for the attackers was minimized with only ten men left behind in the camp. An early morning attack was decided upon as fighting at night wasn't normally accepted due to the teaching of the elders that a spirit could be confused and not get into the afterlife in the proper manner. Dying during the day hours was preferable. However, the Skraelings didn't expect to lose any men now that the numbers were ten to one against the Norsemen. Not knowing how long the party would be split up, the attack was set to occur at the earliest light of sunrise the next morning.

The Norsemen were not prepared. A drowsy guard sat before a bed of glowing embers as the enemy slipped up from behind him silently through the low brush and tall grass.

There were nearly a hundred enemy warriors that came screaming into camp while nine of the ten men were still wrapped in the canvas coverings they used to ward off mosquitoes.

Stone tomahawks quickly dispatched every white man within seconds. Many Skraelings warriors were upset because they hadn't been able to even strike a blow before the battle was over. All that was left was to mutilate the bodies and take whatever items were perhaps useful.

That afternoon, even at a distance of two miles, the crew in the boat saw buzzards flying over the campsite and no smoke was present. Bjoro stood on the highest part of the boat to get to the best observation point. He felt ill as they pulled up to the mooring stone at the camp.

The enemy had done their work thoroughly as if wishing to make a point about invaders. Each body had blood sprayed and scattered several feet around it and most of the dead were barely recognizable even to men that had served with them for months.

The remaining crew determined that the Skraelings felt there was no need to conceal their trail as they had left many tracks and packed down vegetation. A large war party had done the hideous deed and it occurred to the Norsemen that they could be waiting to do it again. Therefore, they were all anxious to complete the burial and leave this place of horror.

The King's Guards chopped and loosened the soil with their ceremonial halberds and several men scooped out the earth with anything they could find.

Ivar was told to carve a message on a large gray stone that was lying there on the ground. Father Pettersson told him what to say and gave him some words to use in the writing. Ivar did well with the hammer and chisel and could create the message more rapidly than anyone else. The priest was familiar with symbols from his Cistercian order and so these were used among the runes. Father Pettersson felt these symbols would be recognized by other priests traveling with Norsemen should they find the stone.

Using several chisels and the heaviest hammer, the rock was squared up into a rectangular shape.

Having done that, Ivar began the actual writing on the stone.

8 Goths and 22 Norwegians on exploration journey from Vinland over the West We had camp by 2 skerries one days journey north from this stone   We were and fished one day After we came home found 10 men red with blood and dead Ave Virgo Maria Save from evil

On the side of the stone, he wrote:

Have 10 men by the sea to see after our Ship 14 days journey from this island Year 1362

Even in the midst of the tragedy, Ivar chipped in a code that identified him as the carver. This was done by an alignment of letters that spelled his first name. The priest didn't catch the little hint of vanity displayed as he gave the rock a cursory inspection prior to the burial of the fallen comrades. Ivar had gained some knowledge of writing from a group of monks he had worked for as a child in his hometown and had learned how to chip rocks from them also.

The crew definitely didn't want to spend another night here so the work was rapid. A common pit was scraped out and the bodies were lovingly placed shoulder to shoulder by the few remaining crewmembers. Each man was thinking about their last conversation with the dead and wishing they could turn back time and do this all differently.

Their fear and hatred of the Skraelings had now increased to an overwhelming desire for revenge. In their minds, the enemy was the worst of cowards and fought from behind trees as often as possible out of fear to challenge anyone face-to-face. This manner of warfare was totally foreign to the Norsemen and quite unthinkable. Killing a man in his bedclothes had to indicate a nation of weak cowards and the killers would be at the moral level of poisoners. Despicable!

Even with the extended daylight of the summer, evening twilight overtook them as they were finishing the burial and memorial duties. The old pagan rituals of sending warriors to sea in a burning boat went through their minds as each handful of sand was pitched into the rapidly filling grave. Shorthorn's arms ached from frantically chipping the stone for several hours and the final words had been added so that the stone could stand as a silent sentinel over the final resting places of their shipmates.

The exhausted crew took to their boat as the sun settled in the western sky and the insects and frogs of the night began their chirps and peeps. Fearing to land anywhere ashore, the crew opted to remain in the boat for the night and set a watch to see that the tiny birch boats of the Skraelings didn't torment them.

At sunrise, the crew made the short trip returning to the site of the massacre and saw the stone they had set up was now lying flat on the ground and the cross that had been next to it had been broken. They were only relieved to see that the gravesite hadn't been otherwise disturbed.

The tiny sail on the small craft was set with oarsmen in place and the crew prepared to go back toward the knorr waiting in the great inland sea. Ivar deepened the words on the stone to make them more distinct and was told that the writing was adequate and they had to leave soon.

With heavy hearts, the Norsemen sailed into the river flowing to the north on their first leg of the trip back to Norway and home. The river was slow flowing without rapids or falls and for a lengthy distance, the width of it kept them out of arrow range of the murderous Skraelings. They occasionally could see them flitting on shore between the massive trees of the nearby forest.

As they approached the narrows of the river, they witnessed in dismay that a thick and heavy string of logs had been strung across it, preventing them from proceeding. With so few men as they now had, they could be hours picking the Skraeling-made dam apart.

The dam hadn't been here a few days back as they entered the lake so they knew the manmade floating log pile was contrived to trap them on this river. They realized the width of the river was now scarcely an arrow shot across and there would be Skraelings on both banks ready with bows prepared to dispatch any Norsemen attempting to tear the interfering dam apart.

The Norsemen had no idea of what may lie to the South and were down to less than the necessary amount of men to complete a journey of exploration. To escape this deadly situation, going north was the only option that Bjoro could consider, but they required the boat to do it!

Bjoro also knew attempting the trip to the inland sea on foot would take months and be suicidal.

CHAPTER ELEVEN

Grounded

The Norsemen immediately recognized the hastily formed log dam as a Skraeling trap. They also knew that there was undoubtedly a huge number of the enemy ashore with the plan of unleashing a hailstorm of arrows onto any man attempting to dislodge the logs in order to get the small boat through on its northward journey to their waiting knorr.

As they paused several hundred yards short of the dam, they could see the enemy coming to the shores and racing toward them. Bjoro wisely stopped well short of the dam and gave the crew a few precious moments to turn their craft around and return to the lake upstream.

By furiously rowing, they made the turn in midstream and were having to row against the current when the first of the burning Skraeling arrows began to rain on the wooden deck. Heavy shields of the same type used by their Viking ancestors were placed in a position as to protect the men from the fiery hail of burning missiles. Each arrow had been dipped in pine pitch and burned without being extinguished in flight.

The enemy appeared on both sides of the river and the fiery hailstorm became nearly constant as the mighty men of the North furiously rowed toward the distant lake. The only advantage of the moment was that the rough and slippery shoreline of the river slowed down the racing Skraelings enough so one Norseman could occasionally dip a leather bucket in the water and splash it about to extinguish the numerous fires now burning throughout the wooden boat.

The speed of the small boat astounded the vicious enemy ashore. Their hissing arrows hit the water as well as the boat, making continual thuds and sputterings as the Norse boat picked up speed in their race to the lake. The sounds of the deadly arrows striking the boat diminished abruptly as the mouth of the flowing stream turned into the lake again.

The heavy leather caps favored by the Norsemen had protected two men from serious injury. The shields and thick jackets they had applied as protection earlier when they approached the dam also kept the crew from what could have been certain death. Three men had been wounded as the fiery darts struck exposed arms and legs but the punctures were quite small due to the penetrating power of the arrows having been largely spent in the lengthy flight. However, the burns were painful and could be a problem healing if not appropriately treated.

The priest hastily applied ointments and dressings procured from a small bag that he'd prepared for the trip. His medical knowledge made him one of the most valuable crewmembers in spite of his small stature. The crew marveled at him and thought, "Is there anything Father Carrots does not have knowledge of?"

What could have been a situation in which the entire remaining crew should have been slaughtered turned into a successful escape - but only for a short time. The river entering the lake from the south was even smaller than the northerly running stream. The southern river had been seen to have rapids and small falls so that the chances of escaping that way were nonexistent. The lake, though of fair size could only afford temporary safety.

Bjoro had to make a decision as to what to do and it couldn't include the use of their beloved boat! They would soon have to land and address the hoard of attackers with certain failure being the probable result.

Since the attack had occurred on the northern edge of the lake, the small boat made full speed for the southern edge to give them some distance from the enemy ashore.

Living aboard the tiny craft was impossible for any length of time, so the only hope for escape would be on foot.

"Afoot in enemy territory with no way to get back to the inland sea except to walk?" Bjoro thought.

It took weeks to come by boat with a full crew and now the trip would be months by foot. Hunting and fishing would take a lot of time and facing the Skraelings on a daily basis would undoubtedly cost them lives. Probably all of their lives!

The knorr waiting at the inland sea had been instructed by Bjoro to leave for Norway before the winter ice blocked the waterways. With a short crew of only ten men, the trip would be difficult enough but the season for travel needed to be summer or early fall. Late fall would kill them too if they remained waiting for Bjoro and the rest of the crew.

This risk had been considered prior to taking the rivers south from the great sea of the north. Both groups were now totally on their own and chances of relief or rescue were non-existent and - they were all well aware of it!

Bjoro directed the ship aground on the shoreline of the lake as far south as they could go. The small craft hit the sandy shore roughly and the men piled off taking everything they could easily carry and leaving the rest. They had to travel lightly but too lightly could mean depriving themselves of necessary articles needed for survival in the unfriendly place.

Seven of the ten men were uninjured but even the injured were capable of carrying some articles needed for survival. Kare carried a triple pack that some of the younger members couldn't even lift.

The forest was dangerous to the sea-faring men. Skraelings could be a pebble toss away but still be totally unseen. Norsemen, just as their Viking ancestors, were not fearful of enemies that were visible but the unseen arrows were not the preferred methods of warfare.

Bjoro had been made aware of a large prairie to the west, that he'd noticed as they traveled south in the past weeks. Without having any knowledge of its size, he felt that the chances of survival were greatly increased out there where the enemy would have to attack out in the open.

"At least we'll die fighting with our weapons in our hands," he thought glumly.

By moving as rapidly as they could with the wounded men and heavy loads, they entered the forest hoping to reach the plains soon and perhaps get some relief from the persistent Skraelings. The men were tired and needed rest, but resting would just allow the enemy to gain on them and the need to keep moving was imperative!

Night was falling and the Norsemen saw the reddish glow to the east indicating that their ship was now in flames and that a return to the great inland sea had become even less of a possibility. Making the tiny birch boats that the Skraelings used would take weeks before the entire crew could be moved and weeks were not available to them.

None of the men had expertise in such matters and no Skraeling boats had been available for them to study as they'd only seen them from a distance.

The Norsemen expected the rain of arrows to begin at any moment, as the enemy wasn't weighed down with gear as they were. They had only a three-hour head start.

The situation they felt most apt to occur was that the enemy would attempt to surround them and prevent them from their westward movement. A trap would be set and the hidden bowmen could pick off the invading white men at their leisure. A game of cat and mouse would be played with a horrible conclusion for the Norsemen.

Bjoro had little reason to hope or expect to live beyond the week.

CHAPTER TWELVE

Flight in the Forest

The small group of Norsemen was near to reaching complete exhaustion. Skraelings had tormented the Norsemen ever since they found their other crewmembers brutally slaughtered and now the chase was relentless.

The men of the north were no strangers to death and they had buried comrades before but the recent informal burial of their ten shipmates had made them uneasy. They had always felt to be in control of the situation but this fight wasn't like any they'd ever experienced.

They couldn't rest for more than a moment before an arrow would whistle into their midst. While these swift little missiles had not actually mortally wounded any one, there had been wounds and eventually someone would be severely injured or killed. It was inevitable and fighting back was impossible when the enemy was invisible in the thick forests.

Their boat, which they had arrived in, was burned and sunk by the Skraelings and the northern sea warriors were stranded in unfamiliar forests without any opportunity to escape on the water. They were carrying their weapons and shields as well as a precious sack of tools and other items they had managed to salvage from their small boat.

If the Skraelings would show themselves, they could have a fight and the chances of success for the yellow-haired giants would be greatly multiplied but the need to keep moving from an unseen foe sapped them of their famous warring skills. Even though there were a few bows and several arrows in their arsenal, they were useless until the Norsemen could find a place of protection.

They had been driven in a westerly direction for several hours and the forests seemed to consist of more brush and smaller trees and the prairies were now before them. They'd been unable to eat except for the lichens, leaves and moss they had found mainly on the forest floor and the shady sides of trees and rocks - along with an occasional raw frog. Seamen were no strangers to starvation or hunger but this was taking its toll upon their mighty strength and the enemy was fully aware that their relentless chasing was paying off.

Different tactics would be required if the large white men got into the open areas as sniping with arrows wouldn't be as effective. But, if the Skraelings would wear the men down to where they were too tired to fight, the battle would be won. A strong feeling of revenge was also driving the Norsemen and remembering their shipmates bathed in blood and murdered while sleeping gave the small group of defenders a strong reason to live and fight. The Norsemen were thinking of that situation and were anxious to get into the open area and see if the flitting shadows in the forest had actual bodies - bodies that would suffer greatly from the wrath of the Norsemen. If only they could get close to them.

Upon reaching the plains of shoulder high grass, Bjoro, the captain of the tiny force, saw a small hill in the distance and felt that the men could rest and defend themselves in better fashion once they'd reached its summit. They had not slept for two days and nights and the need for rest was greater than their hunger at this point. As seamen, they had spent long periods of time awake during storms at sea but having to run without rest as they had been doing, took an enormous toll on them and none could ever recall being so totally exhausted. They could not be driven any further. The shoulder high grass would conceal the enemy to some degree but it was far better than the dark woods from which they'd just departed.

The scorching sun was at its zenith and there were few shadows as the tiny group reached the small mound in the prairie and climbed up to the top. Bjoro cursed loudly and the priest uttered a phrase that would have shocked the men if they hadn't all seen the same sight at the same time.

Indian lodges, about a one-hour walk away, appeared on the western side of the hill. Now they had Skraelings on the west as well as the east. Since the village was sizeable, there would be many more enemies to face from that direction.

Their Viking ancestors were not known to lie down and be killed by the enemy and the sagas told of the brave men of the sea standing against the enemy until the last man died a hero's death. The change from the pagan Viking beliefs of old to the Christian faith didn't change their attitude toward death. They didn't fear it and some were even looking forward to it. The Catholic heaven sounded pleasant and it was a good offer.

Seventy to a hundred Skraelings from the forest had followed the tall white men unto the prairie but had not wanted to get too close until evening. Their strategy was to have one Skraeling warrior slip close to the north men and fire arrows until they gave chase and then the fleeing man would draw the pursuing north men into the close range of several other archers. They didn't want the strangers to enjoy any rest so they would occasionally race toward the group at the top of the hill and shriek loudly before darting back to the safety of the other hidden archers.

One of the best archers of the Norsemen was prepared when an enemy warrior came running up the hill and the arrow that the archer released nearly passed through the intruder. The Norsemen even managed a laugh when they saw the reaction to the foiled plan and no other runners approached the tiny encampment.

Their mirth was shortlived as they saw movement in the Skraeling camp to the west. Leaving the small mound to move into the open plains on the north or south was a poor option.

Ivar, (Shorthorn), was the youngest, and unbearded member of the party and was always expected to show respect to the other members of the group. It was also known that his opinions were not taken seriously but this situation was one that every idea would be listened to and discussed. They were all soon to die and if there were any solutions available, the yellow bearded Norsemen would willingly listen.

The brisk westerly wind bent the tall grass over and had sapped the moisture from man and plant. As all the men were attempting to rest before the final battle, the group was totally silent when Shorthorn spoke.

He addressed his brother Bjoro, but all the men listened. When his plan had been submitted, smiles appeared and heads were nodding vigorously in approval. Shorthorn had remarked that the westerly winds were blowing away from them toward the Skraelings who stood between them and the forest.

"Give me a fire starter and a flint," said Shorthorn. "I will then carry a burning torch from a point in the northeast, lighting a wall of fire back to this place. Someone else can crawl unnoticed to the southeast and light a torch there and light a line of fire back here. If

60

another man came with me, he could start fires running to the northwest or even north to surround the Skraelings to the east of us with fire on three sides and that would cause them to reconsider bothering us as we face the other Skraelings to the west of us. A fourth man to light fires to the southeast also would totally eliminate the chance of them getting around us. We could then deal with the western enemy in the open with no one at our backs. This westerly wind is blowing faster than a man can run and the Skraelings will get their cowardly tail feathers scorched."

It was thus decided that two men would crawl a thousand strides to the northeast and two others would go the same distance to the southeast. When reaching that point, they'd make several torches of the long grass and ignite one each and go in opposite directions lighting a line of fires as they ran. As they did that, two more men within the present group would also light a fire just in front of them and run and race toward the oncoming fire starters so that a solid wall of flame would soon be between them and the enemy skraelings.

The four men rapidly crawled from the tiny camp in separate directions. The signal to light the torches would be given from the central location in the camp. The priest and Bjoro counted very slowly to give the men creeping in the grass time to get to their positions.

Two more men crept in the tall grass only five hundred strides from the camp and they would also ignite a solid line of fire so that there would be a line of fire over a mile long within moments. After the fire had been lit, the men that had started the flames could return on the west side of the flames in the grass that had not burned. They all realized that a change in the wind direction would very likely kill them. The seamen, always conscious of the winds, noted that the prevailing winds had been steadily from the west for the past day or so and felt that their chances of survival were quite good – for a change.

At the appointed time, Bjoro and Soren, one of the King's Body Guard, each took a bundle of grass torches, lit them, using flint and metal fire starters, and ran toward the men that had left earlier in both directions firing the prairie grass as they ran. Immediately, flames grew from the assigned points and a line of fire was rapidly growing in the two directions from the encampment of the white men.

Smoke billowed heavenward and flames shot into the air three and four times the height of a man, totally obscuring the view to the east. The harsh wind drove the flames and smoke into the Skraelings faces at a speed faster than any man could run and the Norse were very interested to see if any could survive such punishment. The Skraelings were many thousand strides from the protection of the woods. They had also been without rest for over two days and nights pursuing the Norsemen so were also suffering from severe exhaustion.

The exhausted Norsemen were sitting on their heavy shields looking to the east when Helge, the best archer of the group, yelled, **"Look behind us. Skraelings!"**

The Norsemen spun around as one. They had temporarily forgotten the village behind them and now they were prepared to pay the price of their forgetfulness. There were at least one hundred and fifty lodges there and, if each lodge held at least one fighting man, they'd be outnumbered fifteen to one.

Kare, the Giant, held his axe in one hand and the huge sword in the other. He'd been taught to wait for the shield bearers to accompany him into battle and he anxiously awaited the order to charge. At that point he would become a berserkr and seeing him in battle gave nightmares even to his friends. All the battle shields were held in place as the men of the north prepared to do battle and, in this case, certainly to their death.

Kare didn't seem to realize that this would certainly be the last battle for any of them. His childish mind was preparing his enormous body to eliminate as many of the red skinned men as he could before being dropped with dozens of arrows sticking out of him.

He waved his sword through the tall grass and a swath of cut grass fell effortlessly. The edges of his weapons had been sharpened to have the best edge known to man and the edges sparkled brightly in the sunlight.

CHAPTER THIRTEEN

Encounter with the Mandans

The picture was puzzling. Well over one hundred Skraelings, just out of range, with bows, lances and war clubs stood at the ready. But, approaching them was a small, elderly, dark skinned man with both hands raised in the air indicating a desire to communicate.

Bjoro, as the chief officer of the group, was confused and considered the act to perhaps be a ruse. But, he also realized this was not typical. To send an old man to speak to them would seem to indicate they were not going to attack them. If these Skraelings had been intending to fight, the consequences would have been bad for the Norsemen, being they were so outnumbered. The old man just kept walking toward them in a manner that appeared gentle and certainly not threatening.

The priest stepped up besides Bjoro and remarked, "This Skraeling seems to want to approach us in peace. I suspect he means no harm. Let me speak to him, Bjoro. I'm not a fighting man and if something happens, you will be able to defend yourself with the men." Bjoro looked at the small red-haired man in the black robe and silently nodded.

He realized that the little man of God may be taking his last steps and how they had become great friends in the past two journeys over the North Sea.

"If we offend him there could be a rain of arrows on us, so I will step back and you can talk to this Skraeling," said Bjoro.

"May God protect and defend us," replied the somber priest. He then raised his hands in the same fashion as the old Indian and the two walked toward each other.

The two men met and stood five feet from each other as their eyes made contact. Neither lowered their hands as they attempted to communicate. Whatever they would get across to each other, it certainly wouldn't be done verbally and they both soon came to recognize that fact.

By using gestures to indicate where they were from and who, indeed, the enemy was, it soon became apparent that these Skraelings were also deadly enemies of the Skraelings that had just fled before the fire.

The priest thought, "The enemies' enemy is my friend." It was when the old man made gestures of eating and drinking that the priest felt a release of pressure and immediately trusted the man. He indicated that he needed to talk to the Norsemen before proceeding.

The Norsemen all agreed they felt extremely hungry and severely thirsty as well as totally exhausted. Knowing that they would be easily beaten in battle in this state, they agreed to enter the village and take their chances. They were reassured when they noticed guards posted around the camp and felt they really needed someone friendly in this strange land.

Women of the tribe furnished water carried in large pots to the Norsemen who drank huge amounts of the liquid as dehydration had weakened them to a state that none of them had ever experienced before. Earlier, in the forest, a muddy marsh had provided them with thick brown water filled with mosquito larva on the first day of their escape but there had been nothing since. That had been two days earlier!

The weakened, exhausted men ate meat of an animal that they'd never tasted before and the vegetables were also different. But, after moss, lichens, frogs, bugs and leaves, it was a glorious feast.

A large lodge was provided and the white giants fell asleep immediately. Some members of the tribe sat up nearby to watch the actions of their new allies. The Norsemen's first instinct was to set their own guard but they were totally at the mercy of these strange Skraelings that had so generously cared for them. No man was capable of another hour of being awake so they all slept soundly for the remainder of the day and into the later morning of the next day.

As each white man came to life and left the lodge, the smell of cooking caused their nostrils to flair. The smell was better than anything they had smelled since leaving Iceland. Small fires dotted the camp as the women prepared a number of their native specialties to offer the tall, yellow-haired strangers.

Even as the Norsemen totally enjoyed their meals, they took note of the fact that all of the village's men had weapons nearby and this concerned and interested them. Were these tools of war meant for use against them? The fact that the Skraelings didn't demand their weapons caused them to feel reassured. Rather, they allowed them to keep them all and only looked upon them with interest and with no sign of malice.

"Who are these people and what do they have in mind?" was a question that the men of the north asked each other repeatedly.

The men of the tribe were well muscled, quite tall and appeared good-natured. However, it wasn't the Skraeling men that interested the Norsemen the most.

The ladies were graceful, lithe and well proportioned. Their facial structure was most pleasant and they all displayed beautiful teeth quite unlike so many of the women of Europe. They also tended to be clean and modest. Smiles seem to come naturally to them and their demeanor was pleasing to the men of the north. The fact that both men and women wore nothing from the waist upwards didn't miss the sailors' attention either!

Shorthorn immediately thought of the "scowler" back in Norway and how she tended to compare poorly with these Skraelings ladies. He'd only been here one day and already was feeling comfortable. He noticed that the girls walked well out of their way to get a better look at the beardless young man - and to give him a better look at them!

Ivar, the only Norse without a beard, was also beginning to enjoy the new experience!

A council had been held on the third night following the Norse and Mandan meeting on the plains. All of the chiefs sat on the east side of a lodge and the Norsemen were given the west side, which is the place of honor in the culture.

Not too much information was transmitted that night other than Torowa indicating, largely by gesture, that the Norsemen would be welcome to come into the camp with them and would be provided shelter and food as guests of the tribe. The priest interpreted the gestures as friendly and welcoming and, in turn, gave symbolic gestures of gratitude and pleasure at the kind offer.

Torowa had indicated that the tribe had owed the Norsemen a great favor by routing the invading Skraelings on the fateful day of their meeting. The Mandan had been expecting a huge raid from that group for some weeks and were prepared to defend themselves. They also knew that the losses would have been tremendous, the women and children would have been taken captive and many of their men slaughtered in a fight. Many of the eastern woodland tribes hated the Mandan and would join, at any opportunity, an attack upon them.

The fact that only seven unwounded men had caused the one hundred attackers to run frantically back to the forest had surprised the enemy Skraelings. They felt anyone that could fight in such unusual ways should be welcomed into the Mandan society as friends.

Telling this to the Norsemen had taken two hours and, at the end of the evening, both sides seem to understand what Torowa was attempting to communicate. He seemed to think that the men from across the water would make good neighbors.

Three weeks quickly passed in the camp of the Mandan and the strangers were feeling safe and secure among the generous natives. All the members of the tribe treated them with respect and honor at all times.

Each Norseman seemed to find a group that interested him the most and they would associate with that group. They then became familiar with that portion of the tribe's culture.

Father Carrots found his place with the leaders and shamen of the Mandan. His ability to learn languages made the most common words of the Indian tongue slip from his mouth easily within a few days. He also spoke Latin and several European tongues as well as ancient Greek and Hebrew. Rapidly getting past the mere greetings and most common parts of speech, the priest was capable of carrying on simple conversations in less than a month.

Even though he was soon acting as interpreter for the Norsemen, they had all picked up a considerable amount of the necessary words that pertained to everyday life. Having a patient and understanding nature, Father Carrots was soon deeply into the teaching and learning scene of the tribe and contributed greatly to the wisdom of the already well-educated tribe.

The elderly leader that had greeted them on the burning plains on the day they'd chased off the enemy by fire was named Torowa. It was readily obvious that he was among the leaders, if not the senior chief, in the Mandan council. The young priest and Torowa both realized that there could be a great increase in their wisdom if they could exchange information.

Torowa had been the first to see the Norsemen close up, as he was the one to approach them on the smoky plains. On that first day of acquaintance he met the little man in the black robe. The assumption was that this small man was the actual leader of the strange group and therefore the man to reckon with.

The Norsemen attempted to help the tribe in the daily tribal needs and quickly learned what was needed to keep a tribe of such size functioning properly.

After several months of heavy work in sailing and exploring this new land, the respite was most welcome. The wounded men were healing well and the opportunity to rest had refreshed them all. Having found friendly Skraelings in a land that had seemed so hostile was indeed a very pleasant surprise.

A situation was in the making that would cement the lives of the yellow bearded Norsemen to the Mandans forever.

CHAPTER FOURTEEN

The Battle at the Mandan Camp

The Mandan suspected that the forest tribes would be massing for an attack on them soon. They had suffered a number of attacks ever since they'd arrived at this place after following the buffalo eastward during this past year.

Food for the great animals had become scarce following a locust infestation, drought, and a prairie fire that occurred in a period of just a few years. These disasters had destroyed an enormous area of the plains. Buffalo had been their main source of food for as long as their history had been told and, having the enormous herds depart the region for edible grass, left the tribe in dire straits. They were a large group with little food on which to exist.

This edge of the forest had a few buffalo to hunt, many elk as well as deer so the tribe was again doing well enough. However, the neighboring tribes had proven to be unfriendly and skirmishes were becoming common. The attackers now were from differing tribes that had joined together and the likelihood of peace existing between them was poor. It appeared that other forest tribes combined for the purpose of war with the Mandan.

A white buffalo had been reported to be with the herd that stayed near the forest and that was a sacred omen to the Mandan. This rare phenomenon had only been seen on a few occasions in their entire history and blessings would come to the persons and tribes who actually saw it. To this date, no sight of it had been found but the hope still persisted that this holy sight may be seen.

Another reason for the Mandan tribe to come to this area was the famous place where stone could be found for making pipes. The Mandan had used tobacco pipes for centuries but had never gotten one made of this particular stone. They had only heard of it from traders of other tribes. Pipes of this material would be the prized possessions of any tribe that could make one.

As tribal members had sought out this marvelous stone, the tribe anxiously awaited the opportunity to finally have pipes made of this soft rock. A small group of Mandan had taken a journey to the place of the pipestone to acquire some pieces that could be shaped into the particular pipes that were so valuable for ceremonies. The group returned with the desired material and presented it to the tribe.

The tribal elders had stared in deep disappointment at the samples of the pipestone that had been brought to them for examination. This stone was red!

White bone, white clay or other white material was always to be used for pipes, certainly not red. Never red! Red was the color of blood and not suitable for a symbol of peace. The Mandan wanted to always be known as a peaceful people and their pipes needed to be symbols of their feelings about peace.

Two scouts were sent back to the ancient villages far to the west to see if the buffalo had returned to that area. The report upon their return was favorable in that new grass was growing in abundance following the fires and locusts and the buffalo were once again feeding near the great river. The tribe was relieved to know they could now leave this place and return to the home of their ancestors.

Returning to the middle of the Great Plains was now a definite goal. Dried meat for the trip was needed and the village women were preparing the food in wrapped packages to pull on the poles that were needed for travel. Captured wolves had been domesticated and served to pull small loads stacked on light wooden poles. Everyone was anxious to return to familiar territory and out of range of the vicious forest enemies.

As the tribe was preparing to break down their camp, a scouting party raced back into camp and ran directly to the large council house to address the tribal leaders. Their news was disturbing and extremely urgent.

They reported an enormous group of the enemy forest Skraelings was assembling near the edge of the forest nearest the Mandan encampment. The reason of the gathering was obvious and the Mandan tribe was in deep danger. Since having multiple wives was an accepted practice of most tribes, a woman-stealing raid would be the most probable reason of the group getting organized so close by. The hot-blooded young men dreamed of such an opportunity to not only get wives but to gain honor by killing other men and thereby gaining rank and stature in the tribe.

During such raids, young children could be taken as well, but the men and older boys would be mercilessly slaughtered if the raid went favorably for the enemy. Such atrocities were known to occur, even in the not too distant past!

Moving an entire tribe took some time to organize and the camp was being broken as rapidly as possible when the warning of the enemy approaching was sounded.

Guards were posted on all sides to prevent the Mandan camp from being encircled and attacked. These guards came into camp with the ominous warning that there had been a large number of enemies racing through the deep grass around the northern and southern ends of the camp with obvious intentions of entirely surrounding the Mandan village.

Having lived all their lives in fear of the dreaded prairie fires, the tribe had burned off or removed the tall grass for several hundred paces around the camp. This also proved to be a useful defense against any approaching enemy.

The Mandan had some additional protection by using the heavy buffalo skins of their collapsed lodges as barricades and shields from the vicious arrows of the enemy. The enemy had only the light shields that they carried. Mandan warriors were positioned around the camp on every side to defend the precious children and women of the village. There would be no quarter given by either side and negotiations weren't even a consideration,

As the number of enemy increased in every direction about the camp, the Mandan tribal leaders quickly discussed how the tribe could best be defended and then distributed their fighters in what they determined to be the most efficient manner.

The Norsemen had been largely ignored as there were only nine fighting men and they weren't familiar in the manner in which the Mandan fought.

Bjoro saw the dispersing of the camp's army and realized that the camp would be fighting for their lives and the conclusion could very likely be disastrous.

The heaviest force of the enemy was standing between them and the forest. A rapid charge was probably coming from that point in the next few moments as the force moved slowly toward the camp, saving their energy for the distance that an arrow could effectively cover. There would be hand-to-hand combat and that was in the Viking blood. It had run through the veins of the yellow-bearded Norsemen for centuries.

Yelling to assemble the men of the north into combat formation, Bjoro and Ivar stood, one on each side of the giant, Kare. Using their own large shields to protect him as well as themselves until reaching the arms length needed for fighting, the three men went to the place where they expected the center of the mass of attackers to hit the camp. Now this would be a real battle and the anger and desire for revenge that the Norsemen felt toward the enemy was about to be resolved on the field. This would finally be their kind of a battle.

Kare, the mentally deficient giant, had the ability to totally lose all mental control in battle. Bellowing as an enraged bull and slashing with a giant sized sword in his left hand and a double bitted battle-axe in his right, he was virtually unstoppable until being bled to death. He stood a head taller than any other man with his heavy leather cap making him even look taller. This type of fighter was called a berserkr and sagas bragged of the terrible loss of lives that had occurred as the result of a berserkr turned loose. Stories of berserkrs were told and retold in army camps with awe and every soldier had a deep desire to actually see one in action. Few had and the scene was unforgettable to those witnessing it.

The remaining six men flanked Kare, Ivar and Bjoro with a King's Body Guard on the outer edges. The fierce looking halberds of the King's Body Guard flashed in the sunlight. These huge battleaxes were ceremonial and usually used for parades and during the appearance of the King but they also served the purpose of effectively doing incredible damage if used against another man. Swords were also a part of the Guard's armor and the edges were as sharp as a barber's razor.

The rest of the Norsemen had the heavy double-edged swords that had served their ancestors so well centuries before in the days of raping and pillaging. The double thickness leather shirts and leggings also gave them some additional protection from arrows.

The camp became deathly quiet as the enemy approached to within arrow striking distance.

Enemy warriors carrying long lances and war clubs moved to the front line and waved these hideous weapons decorated with scalps of their foes. Bjoro recalled the scalps he'd seen in the alehouse that had been carried home from this new land with two blond scalps in the grisly collection. He silently prayed that the hair of his shipmates wouldn't ever be so displayed.

Staring at the advancing enemy, they silently waited and stared at the painted figures approaching them.

The Norsemen began singing a battle song that seemed amazingly loud considering that only nine men were singing it. The song was meant to encourage the fighters but also served as the death song that the Vikings of old would sing before perishing in combat. It served to send a feeling of terror into those facing the singers!

The deep, cavernous voices of Bjoro's men sent shivers down the backs of friend and enemy alike!

CHAPTER FIFTEEN

Norsemen Unleashed

The advancing enemy was just yards short of being within arrow range. The center of the advancing Skraelings' line contained several dozen men carrying heavy war clubs that would crush a skull in a single blow as well as lances, decorated with human scalps, that extended their reach and could pierce far more deeply than an arrow.

The greatest honors were bestowed upon any brave that killed a man with a club or lance. The occasion was often recognized by adding an eagle's feather or some other manner of ornamentation to the killer's headdress to indicate his bravery as well as a scalp to his favorite weapon or leggings.

All the men of the enemy facing them in the center of the line with lances and clubs were so decorated, indicating that the attackers were veterans of many battles. Scalps of the many dead were in evidence on the club carrying attackers. The yellow scalps decorating several nearby lances were fresh and obviously from shipmates of the Norsemen. Colorful paint covered the enemy's bodies and faces so that with their line drawing closer, everyone would be too frightened to fight…or so they hoped.

If the Mandan were frightened, they didn't appear to be so. Everything in their lives that they had ever held to be important was at stake and giving their lives was acceptable and expected of them. They stacked their arrows to aid them in rapid fire and had clubs, knives and spears at the ready. A few feet more and the rain of arrows would begin.

When the enemy attacked, they had every other man shooting so that there were constantly dozens of the deadly missiles hitting the places where the Mandan were standing behind heavy shields of buffalo hide and wooden poles.

The Norsemen remained behind their full-length shields and the constant thudding reminded them of possible death only inches away. Once the club wielding Skraelings reached the Norsemen and their arrows would stop striking them, the enemy figured their clubmen and lancers would finish the work by crushing the skulls of the pathetically few foreigners or impaling them on the wicked spears.

At the very second that the arrows stopped hitting the Norse shields, Bjoro yelled at Kare, "**Attack without mercy and kill them all.**"

With a horrifying bellow that sent chills down the spines of anyone within hearing distance, the huge bearded giant broke out from the protection of the shields. In the next move that he made, he swung his heavy axe unto an enemy nearest to him, causing the man to be neatly split in half!

Everyone was expecting the Norse to be immediately overpowered and to fall dead in a heartbeat but the oncoming club-bearing enemy had raced into the most deadly battle situation that any of them had ever imagined. The arrows had stopped falling as the amazed attackers watched their bravest and best warriors fall before the huge bearded man and his companions. Within moments of the beginning of battle, all the attackers with clubs and lances lay scattered, bleeding at the feet of the Norsemen. Several with limbs totally severed.

The shields were immediately lifted and the berserkr calmed and once again was protected by the shields of the men on either side of him. Having no hand-to-hand fighting to do, the Norsemen stepped backward into the camp and behind the heavy walls of buffalo hide.

Except for an arrow totally piercing the calf of Kare's leg, no arrows had found their mark in the white men. Dozens of arrows were pulled from the shields and given to the archers of the camp to fire back at the intruders.

Kare looked with some amount of surprise at the wicked splinter that had pierced him and, if he suffered any pain, he didn't indicate it at all. It is said that berserkers feel no pain while in action and that appeared to be the case with Kare.

Torowa and the priest attended to Kare and carefully cut the head off the arrow and pulled the projectile out leaving a small but dangerous appearing wound. Torowa had an ointment that he forced into the wound and then bound it with a strip of thin leather.

Having found shelter, the Mandans realized they had suffered very few casualties from arrows. However, a serious blow had been dealt to the intruders who had expected an easy victory after the club wielders and lancers entered the Mandan camp.

Seeing their heroes chopped into pieces had caused a rapid drop in the enthusiasm of the enemy and none were willing to face the Norsemen again, especially with a club or spear.

The sun was sinking into the western sky and the enemy, like most tribes, didn't like to fight after dark. The attackers had envisioned a quick and certain victory so they were totally unprepared for what had happened. Their attack failed miserably and the entire group lost the desire to proceed after their losses had far exceeded what they'd expected.

They would have liked to retrieve the bodies of their fallen but any man getting within arrow striking distance would fall with several Mandan arrows in his body. They hadn't realized the Mandan tribe had become expert in long distance shots, as buffalo had been their main food for centuries. Fighting on the plains was totally different than the forest and the forest tribes soon saw the futility of pursuing this plain tribe.

The story of what had happened that day would be repeated thousands of times in the following years around countless fires of many nations.

The next morning, the village was prepared to depart but waited until guards had been sent out in every direction to assure that the attackers had indeed lost their appetite for revenge.

The war clubs of the enemy fallen were taken and any found with scalps on their possessions were scalped themselves to indicate that they were not respected by the Mandan. The enemy scalps were discarded once the tribe had entered the tall grass prairie. The Yellow scalps found on several lances were buried with a solemn prayer by the red-haired priest and the Norsemen stood with caps off and bowed heads.

For traveling, two long poles would be tied together at one end and separated by about two feet at the other end and belongings would be packed in between the poles as they were pulled along. Wolves they had tamed were harnessed and trained to pull these strange devices to haul loads for the Mandan. With weeks of travel awaiting them, they departed for their homeland with the newest members of the tribe traveling with them. The Norsemen!

Bjoro and his crew knew that certain death awaited them if they remained in this area, as the forest Skraelings would need revenge to keep their honor intact.

Many families of the forest Skraelings had suffered losses during the hand-to-hand combat with the giants from the north and they did not want to go through anything similar to that again. But, they did want to see the Norsemen dead.

The plains seemed endless as day after day and week after week passed with nothing changing in the distance or for hundreds of hours behind them. It strongly reminded the sailors of the seas that they'd traveled for so long. The same grassy rolling hills appeared with occasional packed down grass and places that the buffalo had passed over. Those great animals were seen from time to time during the trip and a hunt was organized to get a few to supplement the diminishing dried meat.

Since the Norsemen weren't familiar with hunting game this large, they were only allowed to get within two thousand paces to observe as the experienced hunters prepared by covering themselves with the skins of buffalo and cautiously slipping closer and nearer to the herd.

At a point very close to the herd, four archers stood up and fired arrows into the sides of two young females. As they bellowed, the men raced toward them with spears to finish them off. A large bull stood a distance off facing them as the herd ran away and, after they had gone, he followed in their path. A full-grown bull's anger wasn't something that a man wanted to face. There were no hiding places in the tall grass. An enraged bull had chased more than one Mandan hunter in the past and the consequences were usually severe.

The fresh meat was a treat that everyone in the tribe thoroughly enjoyed, including the guests. The Norse men had assisted in bringing the meat to camp and laughing women deftly carved it into small pieces with the stone equipment that they used with great dexterity.

"If they can work that well with stone tools, what could they do with steel?" The Mask said to Ivar. The men of The Mask's home town, back in the Lapland forests, had developed fine skills in knife making and even as a child, he had assisted with the craft. These skills were to be of great help to his new friends in the future.

Most of the Norsemen were familiar with butchering but this was a new experience watching the women expertly slash and rip at the meat.

Every one was encouraged to eat as much as they wanted because drying wasn't possible and the meat would be spoiled in a few days while traveling. The Norse appreciated the offer and accepted it happily.

"I never ate this good working for old Gunnar back in Norway," remarked the Mask to Shorthorn.

"No, but didn't you eat as much of Old Gunnar's flax as you wanted?" responded the younger man.

Taking another bite, Mask just snorted at him and the rest of the crew grinned at each other. Ivar was now considered a grownup!

The Mandan hunters had something important to report that thrilled and encouraged the entire tribe. The buffalo herd had been seen to have a white member in it. An excellent omen for the tribe!

CHAPTER SIXTEEN

The Heroes' Reward

After weeks of crossing the enormous plains, the Mandans arrived at a place where they had lived for centuries. They now erected lodges and homes rather than the temporary camps they had lived in for the past year. Many of the frames were still standing from their former occupancy and even some were still covered and could be moved into with just sweeping out and cursory repairs.

The larger lodges were capable of keeping a man and up to four wives and several children comfortable and it was a lodge of this type that was built for the Norsemen. Since it was their home, they added a few refinements that reminded them more of their homes in the "Old Country" as they now called the Scandinavian region from which they had originated.

Having their beds off the floor gave them a small taste of home and they also appreciated chairs and tables. Being used to living with each other in close quarters aboard ship and while camping during their river travels, this arrangement didn't seem to cramp them excessively.

Out of deference for their ranks as priest and captain, Bjoro and Father Carrots were given their own lodge to share, which was considerably smaller.

A piece of canvas that had served as a sleeping cover for the Norsemen was hung separating the sleeping areas of Bjoro and Father Carrots, as priests were given extra privacy for prayers and study. It proved to be a good arrangement for everyone.

The Norsemen had displayed, on two dramatic occasions, their bravery and skills in battle before the Mandan. In addition, they had indicated a good knowledge of agriculture and useful skills that were helpful in their camps. The priest's wisdom regarding astronomy and medicine enabled him to quickly become a respected teacher and he was welcomed into the circle of chiefs and shamen early on.

Total silence was expected as he spoke in council, just as would be for the other leaders. Even though he hadn't totally mastered the

Mandan tongue, it was easy for them to understand him through gestures, expressions and the rapidly increasing vocabulary that he could use.

The small red-haired clergyman saw this as an opportunity to save many souls and increase the number of his flock greatly. He knew that he would not only have to maintain, and constantly deserve the respect of the tribe but he would have to show respect for their customs as well. He felt he needed to do this least until the Norsemen were accepted as welcome guests, or even members, of the Mandan tribe.

If it hadn't been for the blessing of having these gracious hosts provided for them by a loving providence, the men of his group would have their body parts decorating the leggings and lances of the enemy by now. He was not about to be offensive in any manner as his nature had always been to gently guide the ungodly into righteousness rather than to force anyone.

His treatment of the Norse crew was considerably harsher but they were all from Christian homes and had from a young age known right from wrong. They respected the fearless and strong measures that the good monk had provided for them. Any deviation from the teachings of the Catholic Church would immediately bring a sound scolding and warning from the black-clad priest.

A few months had passed and the light-skinned giants moved freely and easily among their hosts. Genuine friendships had developed to the point of asking for favors from each other. At first the favors were just to start fires with the wonderful fire-starting metals and flints that the giants used. The intermixing increased with each passing day and the crew was often invited to the hunts and explorations, which were a part of the Skraelings' life. When it had been determined by both sides that none of them seemed to possess demons or display evil tendencies, the relationship made a positive change.

The Skraeling council met one day, without inviting the priest. The tribal heads felt they needed to discuss some very important subjects.

It had long been a Mandan practice to ask a proven hero to have intercourse with the wives of other tribal members so that the desired characteristics of that man would be introduced to that portion of the tribe. They felt this practice strengthened the tribe and also introduced new bloodlines. This was the subject to be thoroughly discussed as to which visitor should become a partner for which wife. A Mandan could have up to four wives. Any, or all, wives may be expected to bear the hero's children.

All of the tall, strong and brave men of the north possessed greatly desired traits. The discussion determined that each man should be provided with several of the tribal wives over a period of months so that all the next crop of desired children would be mixed with the visitors blood.

The greatest argument, however, was to see which wife or wives should spend a night with the little red-haired priest. He was much smaller than the other Norsemen and even smaller than most Skraelings. He hadn't displayed any strength or skills in battle and was never involved in any tests or games of strength.

While his skills in astronomy, healing and healthy living were considerable, few of the men wanted those characteristics entered into their own families but agreed that these traits were needed in the tribe. The Mandan had no knowledge of the priest's celibacy and were afraid that he would be deeply offended by not being asked to participate since the rest of the crew would be asked.

Old Torowa saw the situation from a different angle and recognized the leadership qualities in the priest as well as the mastery of healing arts and other magic and wisdom that the priest possessed. The old man saw traits that would keep the tribe healthy and free of dangerous entanglements that result from poor reasoning. He wanted those traits to live in the Mandan and the young priest possessed them and - they needed to be shared! He expressed these feelings in the council but each man was allowed to ask the hero of his choice to sleep with his wives and Father Carrots wasn't greatly desired as were the other Norsemen.

Torowa's only wife had died six winters ago and there remained in his lodge only his daughter, Born Under The Plum Blossoms, and himself. Blossom, as she was usually called, was his only remaining child and she took care of the old man's lodge and wasn't married. Torowa considered the problem of the priest and felt his greatest obligation was to the Mandan tribe and, secondly, to his daughter.

Blossom was unusually attractive but her intelligence scared away any suitors. It would immediately become apparent that she was far brighter than the young man courting her and few wanted to live with such a challenge. She made no attempt to charm them by acting silly as the other maids tended to do while being courted.

Blossom asked questions that only the leaders of the tribe would be expected to know the answers to and would then explain to the embarrassed and intimidated young man why these questions were important. Then she would offer several solutions while the suitor squirmed and fidgeted. Desired skills possessed by Mandan women did not include deep thinking and, even though Blossom had all the skills to operate a lodge well, she became bored at mundane tasks and preferred to discuss more abstract things with the wise elders of the group. Therefore, it was at a rather young age that the elders realized that Blossom could provide intelligent answers to serious questions and began to welcome her into their councils.

Few braves returned for a second helping of Blossom's incredible wisdom! They continued to enjoy watching her walk through camp and admired her shape and grace but none dared to challenge her in conversation. She was curious about everything and demanded answers to why everything worked in such perfect coordination - until a human disturbed it. To Blossom, everything was a mystery and she was fascinated in finding the answers.

Old Torowa saw his daughter as being a perfect match for the priest.

CHAPTER SEVENTEEN

Torewa's Request to Father Carrots

The decision of the council to allow the tribal men to invite the tall strangers from the north to their lodges to spend the night with their wives passed through the village with the speed of a prairie grass fire. Invitations were extended immediately to the amazed Norsemen. None of the crew expressed reluctance to oblige the Mandan request as they'd been gone from their homes for many months and knew that returning to the motherland was probably out of the question. Some were feeling very comfortable here and didn't have much to return to back over there anyway.

The priest didn't hear about the new situation for a few days but his suspicions were aroused. He knew the crew had been doing something that he may not approve of and suspected that the native ladies were a part of it. His worries were that they would offend the Mandans and anger them by mixing with the ladies and that, under Catholic conditions, would be totally unacceptable. While he felt only a very slight sense of relief at learning the men were committing fornication by invitation, he still disapproved of it but now it would be something that he could address and feel in charge again.

It was while he was preparing a scorching sermon and a severe scolding for the next mass that Torowa and his lovely daughter, Blossom, approached him. The elderly tribal leader sat near the priest and smiled in a brotherly fashion that would put the most disturbed person at ease. The old man began by commenting on the priest's many remarkable qualities that he, the Council and tribe admired so much.

He continued by saying, "Your wisdom of the heavens is a beautiful thing. I've heard you speak of the flashing lights of the northern night with the knowledge of an ancient shaman that had studied the heavens all his many winters. We are fascinated by hearing your thoughts while watching an upside down bird walk headfirst down a tree as only that kind can do and provide a logical explanation as to why they choose to act in such a manner. Your answers to every question are well thought out and clear. You lead your men as a giant would but have only half of the weight and size of some of them and you still command great respect. Bravery and you are not strangers and yet I've witnessed your eyes moisten as a baby child was being born. Your respect for your gods is very impressive but also you show regard for all living things and do no damage to creatures or plants."

The priest, becoming slightly embarrassed as to how the conversation was going, attempted to interject a remark but the raised hand of the elder man showed this was not an acceptable time to do so. That gesture was one used in council and the young priest now recognized it and respected the act by keeping totally silent and totally attentive.

Torowa continued, "Your ability to treat sickness and wounds by using proper substances, medicines, herbs and words has been admired and discussed by many. Your delicate handling of matters of importance as well as your strength of logic to change the course of events has been considered and has been envied by many of us that have spent our lives developing such skills. These are things that make a great nation such as the Mandan - a healthy and growing nation. You number among the very few that can display love and concern for others while bearing the spear of leadership that may cause you to send others to their deaths. You, man dressed in black, have many qualities that the Mandan want and need, not only for now but also for the future generations of our tribe."

The ancient leader of the Mandan nation kept his hand raised as he contemplated his next remarks and the red-haired priest sat solemnly quiet in respect for the old man's time to speak.

"Our nation, the Mandan, is a fine nation of people. However, we are people that would quickly change for the worst if our culture isn't carefully maintained and groomed. We are aware that the wisest and best leaders are those that display traits such as I've seen and mentioned in you. While there are those of our nation that say you are gods, you do not say so. You claim to be men and men are born, live and die. So it appears to be with you.

You cannot be with us forever but you do have something that will give us additional strength and wisdom to make the Mandan a better nation and a better people. We need your blood to flow in us and let your traditions strengthen us as the winters and summers flow past."

Hearing the emotion in the voice of the ancient leader, the priest felt himself wanting to serve these wonderful people for the rest of his life. He had committed himself to the Catholic Church as a child and now felt as he did at that earlier time of his life. The need to serve had never been far from him but it was now welling up and energizing him with a desire to do whatever this respected elder wanted him to do.

He was being asked to serve by those who needed him and the assignment was sincerely from the heart and given in person and not transmitted by Rome or a bishop from afar. He hadn't heard just what it was that the tribe needed from him but he would provide whatever he could for their well being. He had come to truly love these people!

The red-haired priest was glad that it was a cool night as Blossom was very modestly dressed. Mandan women would frequently remove their upper garments on hot days and no one seemed to think anything of it - except the Norsemen. These yellow haired strangers would walk into each other, stumble over their own feet and bump into lodges while staring at the Mandan women that walked about unashamed while being naked from the waist up.

The priest wanted to tell the men to use some self control and stop gawking and acting so stupid but, he had to admit, the situation did distract him too. He knew that he couldn't change the Skraeling customs so he kept silent.

He had been listening to Torowa and that required his full attention but his gaze did occasionally stray over to Blossom, and it bothered him that he enjoyed it so.

CHAPTER EIGHTEEN

A Favor to the Mandan

The young red-haired priest was in a quandary. Would a loving God place him in a situation to test him and the crewmen at a time like this? Their trials had already been enormous and they had tried to be obedient in every instance. He had performed mass every day and offered prayers as was expected of every monk in his order as well as good works and teaching. This trial was not one that he could recall hearing about in the scriptures he'd studied.

Old Torowa, one of the head shamen of the tribe and perhaps the most respected man in the tribe had just humbly asked him for the strangest of favors. To refuse the man would possibly be so insulting that the chance for conversion to Christianity of these lovely people could be lost, not to mention the friendship between the men of the north and the Mandan nation.

The elderly man and his very lovely daughter had asked to have a meeting with the priest and the talk was to be of the most serious nature and importance to the tribe. The older man had explained that the behavior of his group was normally quite gentle but the harsher side had too often appeared. In order to prevent the harsh side from dominating the tribe in the future, he felt this required a balance in the leadership to prevent poor decisions and improper acts from occurring to endanger the future of the group.

It may have been only because of this man's great wisdom and ability to wisely negotiate that the tribe was even alive at this time. He knew his remaining days were few and the other chiefs, good men that they were, had displayed hot blood at times, when there had been options, and only the wise counsel provided by Torowa had prevented catastrophe. It was his responsibility to keep some deep thinkers in the council and Torowa was troubled, as there were so few to choose from.

The Mandan hierarchy was composed of seven levels and each level was determined by the qualities found in the men of the tribe. Very few made it to the seventh level and, once there, those men had the total respect of every member and was given the responsibility of maintaining the entire tribes welfare. All the wisdom of their history was in the minds of these elderly wise men!

To attain that level, Torowa had tortured his body by swinging from ropes tied to sturdy wooden sticks puncturing his breasts until the weight of his body broke them. Not an easy feat for a man of smaller size. He had sat out on the plains fasting for up to nine days without water or food and had danced at many Sun Dances. He had experienced visions. He had given all of his wealth and other goods to those that had less than himself and had devoted his life to the improvement of the Mandan tribe. He had never been heard to speak evil of any man or animal and was revered by many as a god. A genuine smile always seemed to be present on his weathered face.

The request of the old man was simply to have the priest give his daughter a child. Preferably, it would be a boy child so that a wise leader would be provided for the well being of the group. He didn't even ask that the priest marry the girl, although that would have been desirable. He merely wanted to have children of the young red-haired stranger in the tribe to be trained for the position of leader. The custom was to ask a man with great ability or skill to spend a night with the wife of a tribal member so that the talents would be transmitted into the tribe through another link.

Since Torowa no longer had a wife and, even if his wife had been alive, she would have been far too old to bear children. The second reason that the daughter would be an excellent choice was that her superior intelligence would not be wasted in her children and, to have a father such as this man, the children would be pillars of the tribe and certainly great examples and leaders. The Mandan had long known that the combining of good characteristics made a superior person and grooming of marriages was common.

"I cannot do that!" was the first thought of the monk as he listened to the request. However, to his credit, he did not leap to his feet in protest or make any sign of refusal until the ancient shaman completed his argument. That would have been exceedingly impolite and considered terribly rude to treat the highest ranked elder so.

As the old man explained, at great length, what was needed for the tribe to grow in balance and health, the attractive daughter sat next to the blanketed elder and adjusted his blankets as they slipped from the shoulder his raised hand extended from. She did not smile or show the slightest expression during the entire meeting. She just looked at the monk with her hands neatly folded in her lap except to correct her father's garb as it slipped occasionally. The priest could not help but notice the adoration in the girl's eyes for her father. "Such love is certainly of God," thought the monk as the commandment to honor one's parents came into his mind.

The red-haired Norseman knew the customs of the tribe allowed one to just sit quietly and carefully think before responding so he took many minutes to consider the matter and how to present his argument for not accepting the request. He was dismayed as he had considered an appropriate rebuttal and raised his eyes to answer. When his eyes met hers, his mind was swept clean of all answering remarks and he realized that he was in the company of one of the loveliest beings that he'd ever seen. He lowered his hand again and attempted to regain his thoughts.

"The Madonna," was the thought that struck him as he tried not to stare. Her beautiful mind was legendary and he'd often heard squaws remarking that other women should emulate Blossom in everything that they may do.

Her hair hung loosely as she had felt that her appearance should be acceptable to the stranger but not too fancy. While braids were the most common hairstyles of the women, a singular braid or even a tying off of the entire longer hair was occasionally seen throughout the camp. The priest had never had such strong feelings for another human - especially a woman. These feelings he had were not merely lust. He felt she was worth dying for and he would have done so without question.

She'd been known to prefer moderation in her dress and, even though she was skilled in beadwork, she had only well placed beads in a few places on her well-tailored dresses. While she had intentionally made her clothing to fit nicely, she never seemed aware of being envied by the women and lusted after by the men of the village.

Father Carrots made another attempt at answering the request of the old Skraeling leader. He wanted to explain how he could never be a father even though that was his title.

"Too difficult to explain," he thought. "I don't even know if I really know why this is the case." His thoughts went fleeting to a scripture that he'd pondered over that said, "Call no man father."

"Doesn't that apply to me too?" He considered quoting Paul and showing that remaining single was preferable. However, that would apply only if marriage was considered, but it hadn't been emphasized.

His gaze again met hers and the thoughts that had been so clear moments before were now clouded. He felt himself blushing as his eyes drifted over her and this confused him. These were the behaviors of a young buck such as Short Horn but a mature priest should not entertain such feelings and thoughts. "St. Peter had been married and perhaps others had been too." His mind was swirling!

He bowed his head in a short but fervent prayer asking for ways to answer the questions of the old man and his beautiful daughter.

"How do you want me to answer this without being offensive, Lord?" asked the priest. "I know that you do not want us to offend but…I want to do what you'd have me do. WHAT IS IT?"

As the priest raised his head, his answer had been prepared. His mother had decided that he should be a priest but he'd never even been asked about the decision. He'd been aware of the priests and bishops having wives and lovers in spite of their vows and he was determined not ever to do that. When he'd asked that question in discussions with the Bishop, he'd caused some angry red faces to occur and his being sent to a monastery and then on this mission had probably resulted from that occasion. He knew what he needed to do and a priest could not do it this way.

He would renounce his vows and marry Blossom!

CHAPTER NINETEEN

Father Carrot's Last Sermon

The Norsemen were assembled at the Sunday mass and they were feeling the need of hearing something that would enable them to feel a little less ashamed. They had visited the beds of the tribal ladies with the permission and at the request of the Mandan men and with full knowledge of the tribe.

This sort of thing would never have occurred back home and they hadn't ever expected it, especially amongst the Skraelings. They hadn't spoken to Father Pettersson before agreeing to the invitation, as they knew full well what he'd say. Now they wished they had done so but it was too late. The deed was done.

Several of them felt shame for the fact that they didn't feel as ashamed as they should have. This was an unheard of problem.

Their pagan Viking ancestors wouldn't have been troubled about this sort of thing as they raped, pillaged and destroyed as they traveled about the world. But these Norsemen were Christians and the rules had changed. Their black clad priest saw to it that they knew all these rules and they were expected to keep them.

They suspected the sermon would be a strong warning with a listing of penalties for their sins and their weak willingness to accept the tribe's invitation to increase the numbers of the Mandan. This would not be a pleasant experience, they were all certain of that! They all sat with their heads bowed awaiting the admonition that was certain to come.

The dark sunken eyes of the young monk indicated that he hadn't slept enough and the men were aware of his situation and felt sorry they had put him through this trial.

None of them were in the slightest bit aware of his deep questions regarding the daughter of the elderly chief and what was troubling him in regards to his own rules of living. Priests gave out as much personal information as they wished and to ask would be impertinent.

The service began in the usual fashion and the tiny congregation dreaded what they were sure was to come as they mentally prepared themselves for the chastising that was to follow. They had willingly acted as pagans and hadn't considered the consequences of their deeds. Father Carrots would see that they were properly reminded of their carelessness.

They were somewhat surprised at the gentle manner of the priest as he began the portion of the service that would normally contain the threats and warnings. While he pointed out the sins of adultery and fornication, he remarked that the laws prohibiting them were appropriate in the societies from which they had come from and that this was a totally different culture. As Christians and good Catholics, they should remember that these laws were for all men but it was their job to teach the Skraelings about them.

"We are not apt to ever see the lands of our origin again," stated the priest in his opening statement. "We realized the possibilities of this before we departed the old land and were all prepared to come to this new world and die here, if that is God's will."

"Our good King Magnus sent us to find brothers in faith that may have been lost and needed assistance but he knew the trip could end in a manner such as we are now experiencing. Our desire to honor the King should only be second to our desire to honor God and that is still where we remain today. The Crown prefers that we live our lives as good examples and follow God's laws wherever we may be."

He went on to remark, "There are some situations that make this excursion unique and different from all others. Death was our companion in this new land and it was only due to the miracle of the Mandan people being in a place they had never traveled to before that we are alive and here today. Had we changed our course in the slightest manner, we could have suffered the same fate of our brothers, who perished at the hands of our enemies. However, we were spared. Why did that occur? Was it our great wisdom and ability to survive that we are here today or did God have a purpose for us that allowed us to live and breathe as we are now doing?

"We all recall the panic and fear that we felt as we ran through the forest with death within sight and no hope of survival.... But we live! And here among the friendly Mandan, we live well with no hunger or thirst. Beside that, we have protection from the enemies of man and elements. Could we doubt that God is protecting us? Again,

I have to ask why would He want us to continue when the mission we were on has failed? I suggest that there is more for us to do and we need to do it, whatever His will may be."

The sermon continued, "God has made it plain that it is not good for man to live alone. He also said that man is to reproduce and provide children. He makes it plain that marriage is required before a man and woman should have sexual involvement.

"Even this Mandan culture recognizes marriage with men having up to four wives. They also have the option of having their bloodlines increased by their invitation to outside men of great respect. While they readily accept us and give us honor, it would be best in God's eyes to marry the woman that you share your bed with in order to keep within God's laws.

"We are going to remain with the Mandan as long as they will allow us to enjoy the comforts of their camps. Therefore, it is in our best interests to become more as they are without becoming pagan.

"Before I was assigned to come on this voyage, I had expressed questions to those in authority over me in the church resulting in turmoil and embarrassment to men that I was compelled to obey. I felt it was my duty to show the differences between the Holy Scriptures and what had become common in the church. Such changes from what was written were to be only known by a literate few of the church leaders and not to be announced to the masses. I could see that God's laws and way of life should be available to everyman and the leadership was to provide guidance as needed but not to govern by manmade rules."

"I know and love God and his Son, Jesus the Christ, but I do not feel that their way of life has been properly taught or lived under the church as it has evolved. I've seen excesses by those who were supposed to be servants to the masses as all priests are. I've noted greed from which bread was taken from the mouths of the families working and given to an organization that claimed to be doing God's will - but wasn't. There have been many things added to the original books that were placed there by men seeking to gain power over the common people. There was, however, no man to defend the original writings or those suffering from church taxes and bullying. I have seen the old books that spoke the truth burned as heresy.

"This manner of thinking has disturbed many other priests and brothers who have witnessed excesses, tyranny and greediness in what should be an organization made to honor and serve the Almighty. It has become a place where vows are taken lightly and largely ignored after being said."

"I would happily die as a servant doing God's will and that has been my prayer since entering this life as a priest and servant of God. It is still my prayer and I will continue to serve Him and you to my dying day but I cannot act in a manner that I no longer find to be the true faith as I read it in the Holy Scriptures. I will work as one of you, doing whatever is required to earn my daily bread, and will still serve as a teacher of God's ways as long as you wish to have me in such a position.

"Just as the scriptures clearly state, 'Call no man father,' I would ask you to refrain from calling me by that title in the future. My name is Conn and I will answer to that. The title 'Father Pettersson' is no longer appropriate. Perhaps you would be so kind as to retire the title 'Father Carrots' also," he said as he paused with a smile...his first smile that day.

He continued by saying, "I want to be a loving servant to you and God. I will counsel, advise, and minister to all as I have been given the strength to do. If requested, I will perform weekly church services, perform marriages before God, baptize, listen to any whose hearts need to confess, assist at deaths and burials and any other acts that may be useful in God's work."

"God has not abandoned us nor is he apt to do so. He has placed us in a group of people that seem to have many of the same ideas as we do in so far as being peaceful and loving toward each other.

"We must not become pagan and we will not act in a manner that gives us advantage over others nor appear to be greater. The Mandans have given us high honor and recognition but that is only due to our slightly advanced culture and not our own merit. We must remember that."

Conn then made a symbolic gesture of a cross over the Norsemen and closed by saying, "May Jesus walk with us and God guide every thought and act we do in our new place on this new land. May our presence here be a blessing on these people for ages to come. Amen."

CHAPTER TWENTY

Bjoro and Solveig

Life in the Mandan camp was quiet and peaceful as the Norsemen were accepting the realization that they would now be calling this strange place home and they would never return to the fjords and fields of their homelands. They did not seem to be greatly troubled by that idea and they now looked at how they could best adapt to this different way of life.

The Mandan tribe had given them security and a welcoming they would have never expected to get in this wild land of enemies and sudden death to white men. Sagas dating back centuries had always strongly warned the sailors of the perils of landing on these shores and of the horrible fate met by many of their ancestors who had attempted to explore the coasts and inland rivers of this immense place.

Bjoro's thoughts of home also included the bride that his father had chosen for him. She happened to be a scowling sister of the 'Scowler' family that his father had picked for Ivar. He smiled to himself as the thought occurred to him that choosing women of that unpleasant family for his sons to marry had driven two of his sons to the sea.

Perhaps father just wanted the boys out of the nest and knew that this threat of marriage would certainly do it. More likely, however, his father just wanted to improve the lives of his sons and his family by marrying into a well-established and wealthy family.

The desires of the young couple were not considered as the common belief that the elders were better prepared at making such decisions than the younger was rarely disputed.

Bjoro had been unsure about his course in life until Sir Paul accepted him as a deck hand on a voyage to the Mediterranean for trading in Italy and Greece. That trip, he remembered, was pivotal in his life and the life of a merchant in the 'Scowlers' family no longer stood a chance of being a vocation for him.

Sailing and learning from Captain Paul Knutson had been an excellent education for the young Norse. Not only had he worked with men of other nations and become familiar with their languages, but he had gotten to know the fundamentals of trade and transport as well as reading and writing under the constant tutelage of Sir Paul. The captain was literate and appreciated the written word as a step toward success.

As the Captain came to recognize Bjoro's talents and abilities, more responsibility was given to him. He'd been worked hard but was never distant from the expertise of the aging master. His cheerful personality made him a favorite of both the officers and crew and any difficult problems were soon directed to him for correction. Everything from a tempest at sea to a hardnosed merchant was thrown to him in those important years of training.

Sir Paul attempted to present every sort of difficulty to Bjoro so his education would qualify him for the highest ranks of the King's service or the Norse maritime trading. Bjoro remembered when an actual situation didn't present itself, the elder teacher intentionally created one to see what his actions would be. Navigation, ship maintenance and handling, sailing in storms and high winds, fighting with pirates and hand-to hand combat were all included in the training of the young man and always under the attentive eye of the senior instructor. Basic reading skills were fit into the program and well accepted by the young First Mate.

Although it wasn't mentioned, Bjoro's arranged marriage had also entered into the equation and would not have fit handily into the plans of Sir Paul. A shipmaster needed freedom to travel for months or years at a time with something pleasant to come home to at the end of a voyage - like his own wife, Margret. Sir Paul's heavy yellow whiskers hid most of his expressions but when the subject of his wife, Margret, arose, everyone knew Sir Paul would be smiling widely! His eyes would crinkle to the point of almost being shut and the laugh lines clearly displayed his emotions.

Bjoro had met Margret and knew that she was the greatest prize the elder sailor had ever sought. She was not only an exceptionally pretty lady and had all of the qualities a man of his rank and stature needed in a wife but it was her personality that caused everyone to stand in awe when first meeting her. She loved everyone and she could put a person at ease during the first words leaving from her mouth. She was easily the most popular person in that part of Norway, in Bjoro's opinion.

Sir Paul was the envy of anyone who had ever met Margret and he never failed to show his adoration for her. Every trip had a gift for her in the hold of the ship and she was always the first person the captain went to see upon docking at the quays of his hometown.

After meeting Margret Knutson, Bjoro knew exactly what womanly qualities he wanted to find in a wife. A woman that had even half of Margret's qualities would have been exceptional and he knew he would never be satisfied until he found someone very much like her. He'd fully expected to search for years to find someone even strongly similar to Margret and...it seemed as if he never would. Even if it took his entire lifetime, he intended to continue his search until that special woman appeared.

Now he was in a Skraeling camp and had no hope of ever going back to the old country. But, that particular thought didn't bother him a bit.

Now he found it nearly unimaginable that he was looking at such a woman as Sir Paul's Margret from across a small fire in the middle of the Skraeling camp and she was looking back at him - and smiling! At him!

Conn, formerly Father Carrots, had performed the marriage ceremony four days ago and Bjoro now had exactly the type of wife Sir Paul had recommended. Bjoro smiled back at his new wife. He felt no man could have been happier than he was at this moment.

Her Indian name was lengthy and descriptive of the weather at the time of her birth. Bjoro, however, had always liked the Norse girls' name "Solveig," as it had been his mother's, and happily applied it to his new bride with her cheerful permission.

Sir Paul would have heartily approved. Bjoro had found his own Margret...with Solveig! Bjoro could easily imagine Sir Paul's eyes crinkling up with happiness if he could have heard of this beautiful and loving arrangement his favorite student had created for himself. His eyes would have crinkled even more had he been made aware of the fact Bjoro's first son would be named Paul in his honor.

Bjoro lifted a flask of hot dandelion tea to his former master's memory.

Several elderly ladies sitting at a nearby fire smiled knowingly at each other as Bjoro stood and circled the fire to be at Solveig's side.

Brushing his fingers along her cheeks and chin, he reached for her with his other hand to assist her to stand. They then slowly and silently walked the short distance toward their lodge while gazing in each other's eyes.

After they'd entered the lodge, one of the nearby ladies raised her hand with several fingers extended as she'd been carefully counting how many times the young couple had repeated those actions of returning to their bed that day. The rest of the group cheerfully acknowledged her and silently bobbed their heads in approval and amusement. All Mandans laughed easily but this event would be a cause for laughter for decades to come.

These Norsemen were good for a lot of laughs! It was nice having them around!

CHAPTER TWENTY-ONE

Life in the Mandan Village

Skraelings from the various tribes about them occasionally had skirmishes with the Mandan. The Norsemen now felt to be a part of the tribe that had befriended and provided for them and they fought willingly and fiercely to protect their friends' property from any and all comers.

The foreign tribes soon realized that the Mandan had a weapon they couldn't compete against in hand-to-hand struggle. The weapon was the enormous giant who would race fiercely screaming toward any apparent enemy, swinging a specially crafted axe over his head and splitting asunder any enemy that remained within his range. Two of his white skinned comrades raced next to him carrying large shields to protect him as both of his hands contained weapons of carnage unknown to them or any other enemy ever encountered.

While the enemy attempted to shower him with arrows, the light, but extremely efficient shields, caught the light arrows and prevented damage to the protected giant as well as the soldiers carrying them,

On one occasion, an arrow did strike the giant on the bicep of his arm but it never slowed his attack in the slightest, even though it had totally penetrated his enormous muscle and was protruding out the back. He wasn't even aware of the painful injury until the enemy Skraelings, having observed the arrow strike, raced away in terror.

Father Carrots, now called Conn, while skilled in medicine and healing, humbly and willingly accepted the medicines from the shamans of the Mandan and appreciated the success of the healing.

The "medicine men" (and women) of the tribe wanted to do a healing ceremony for their now enormously respected "secret weapon" but the former priest didn't permit that.

The tribe did, however, build a steam hut for the large man to enter and cleanse himself. The priest didn't object to that even though the concept of cleanliness and healing wasn't a consideration for most of the world. Bathing was considered unfashionable and even unhealthy by much of Europe.

Due to his fascination of other cultures, Conn recognized the fact that the more hygienic some groups were, the less diseases troubled them. He'd written this information in his books of notes and recalled it frequently and wondered why this phenomenon repeated itself. He also commented in his notes that the Mandan tribe usually slept naked and he wondered if that wasn't something that attributed to the well being of the tribe. The Norse didn't waste time developing that sleeping habit and wondered if the temperatures back in the "old country" caused everyone to dress for slumber rather than undress.

In addition, Conn had preserved the dandelion seeds from the patch found in Vinland planted by their Viking ancestors. The precious parcel of seeds had been carried in a tiny pouch the Norsemen used for their most valued possessions and, in the case of the former priest, they shared the space only with his cherished magnifying glass.

He had planted them near the Mandan village and was looking forward to the wonderful remedies provided by the bright little yellow flowers. The miraculous cures were used back home for nearly every ailment known and not possessing this plant would cause a near panic in anyone lacking it. He'd been to places that the dandelion patch had been carefully protected due to the demand for the cures it provided.

Unbeknownst to the Norsemen, the Mandan shaman, of which several were women, left the camp and had a healing ceremony and dance for Kare the Giant. They later sprinkled him with the sacred pollens and herbs while Conn was elsewhere. Other than deep dimples on his arm, both in front and back, the wound was soon closed and infection free to the amazement of Conn and the Norse crew. Nasty festering wounds leaving ugly scars had been a part of their heritage and were not missed if they could be replaced by rapid and clean healing.

Mask, the Finnish crewman, especially appreciated the steam bath as it reminded him of the saunas of his younger years back in what was to eventually become Finland. Other crewmembers came to use the steam room and it became a part of their lives as they found it to be not only cleansing but also relaxing and refreshing. With the positive remarks about Mask's saunas back home and the Skraelings' fondness and frequent use of the baths, the men of the north eventually made bathing a habit.

The absence of the human stench was a welcome change. They had gotten used to it in their lives to the point they didn't realize how unpleasant it was until they no longer suffered from it.

The Mandans pointed out that wild game was easier to approach when hunting after a steam bath and the inquisitive Norsemen did not miss the logic of this fact.

The tribal members usually ate well in the Mandan village and the diet of buffalo and a variety of vegetables was well accepted. A large variety of birds, rabbits, prairie dogs and other small game contributed to their diet with seasonal changes. On one occasion a fishing trip had gone well and a large amount of fish was prepared in a manner that had been popular in Norway.

By processing the fish with lye, the Norsemen were happy to offer the tribe a dish that was popular in their country, called lutefisk.

Torowa, the wise old chief sniffed the delicacy before tasting it and looked quizzically at the Norsemen and remarked, "The Mandan usually want to eat the fish before it spoils."

He only consumed it to prevent offending the white men. That method of preparing fish never became popular in the tribe even though the strange yellow haired giants prepared it for themselves frequently.

The Skraelings, Mandan or others, didn't have private ownership of land as Norsemen were accustomed to. All of the surrounding lands were Mandan and could be used for planting, housing or hunting by any tribal member. Other than the areas directly under and around their lodges, the land was communal.

The Norsemen missed the longhouses of home and considered how to acquire the proper material to build one in the Skraeling village. Shortage of lumber prevented the Norsemen from building houses, as they knew them in the old country. They did, however, build a church from the few trees available but took care to see that seedlings of more trees were protected.

Soil covered skin dwellings were preferred by the Indians. Quick and easy to construct, such shelters were strong and could be left as the tribe moved about and easily rebuilt if needed. The Mandan seemed to prefer having the lodges built very close to each other with only enough space between them to walk.

In addition, they were warm in winter and cool in summer and easily cleaned.

There were several islands of good standing timber and parties were sent out to float rafts of logs back to the village so a building could be constructed. All the sailors were experienced carpenters and craftsmen in various trades and the task was eagerly anticipated.

Since there wasn't any likelihood of meeting the other Norse ships before winter, there was no argument against making a suitable building that could be used for daily living as well as church services and meetings. A large building for gatherings was desired and built in the rectangle shape of the functional churches that they were used to.

The Indians were very interested in the industrious foreigners and contributed to the labor of chopping, floating and construction. Eventually, even a moat was dug around the camp to increase the security of the tribe

CHAPTER TWENTY-TWO

Hidatsa Visitors

The lead men of the Skraeling village were not given their respected positions for being just war chiefs. All the leaders were men of advanced age and were well loved by the villagers.

Any problem that required wisdom was immediately brought before one of the elders and, if an immediate answer wasn't given, several other leaders were invited to consider the matter and provide assistance. Included in the council were numerous shamen (of whom several were women) and discussions would last until a logical answer could be provided.

The Norsemen were amazed as to how the humorous fun-loving old men could become so serious when in council. If a council of war was required, the ancient leaders were up to the task and wisely counted the cost of how to get out of the bad situation with the least amount of harm to the tribe.

If a war situation was hopeless, they would readily consider surrendering and paying the required cost to the invaders, but - that never occurred. Thanks to the great wisdom of these men, enemies had always realized their losses would be too severe if they should invade Mandan territory.

Until the ancestors of the feared Vikings had arrived, there had been an occasional raid by various tribes into the Mandan hunting territory but the arrival of the mysterious giants changed that. Hot-blooded braves of nearby nations could gain immediate fame by "counting coup" as the practice was later to be called.

While they had no desire to have a war with the Mandan, the young braves of other tribes each had a desire to be known as "the man that had touched the giant and lived." It was a task that would place them into legendary figures for perhaps centuries to come and many a young brave considered being called the "Man That Touched Giants and Lived."

Many were the young men that crawled to their blankets at night scheming as to how to do this task with a large audience observing as witnesses and how the women would ask him to repeat the story over and over as he chose which of them to be his. Having achieved this victory, a decoration would be prominently displayed on his clothing for all to see and know that he'd accomplished something important in meeting an enemy. When a hero appeared at dances wearing those hard-earned feathers and painted designs on his clothing, the camp would display great respect and honor to the wearer. Thousands of young braves probably fell asleep smiling with these thoughts being incorporated into their dreams.

One day alert Mandan sentries became alarmed as they studied the sand they'd swept clear of any marks on the previous night. They now reported of strange moccasin prints being seen in the vicinity of the outlying fields and even to nearly within an arrow shot of the village during the past evening.

This event raised great concern to everyone, especially the elders. A council was hurriedly called and discussions were held as to what kind of preparation needed to be considered.

The elders studied the tracks by measuring the stride, length and width, as well as the type of moccasin, depth of the imprint, and position of the invader.

"Hidatsa!"

Everyone recognized the unmistakable sign of their lifelong enemies. They then considered the purpose of the surreptitious visits and the conclusions were that their tribe's strength was being measured. This would indicate a possible attack. But, when the greatest interest of the "visitors" seemed to be in the location of the Norsemen, the old men smiled at each other and one said, "Someone wants to count coup and get a feather." There was unanimous nodding of heads affirming that fact from all the council.

In that an attack would surely cause many deaths for the attackers, it wasn't likely that the camp was in danger. One member of the enemy may slip into the outer edges of the camp but a larger force would certainly be seen, as the Mandan had not lowered their guard in many years.

The oldest of the Mandan elders had all been young men when a Hidatsa raiding party had once raced into camp and stolen three women. They had escaped without so much as an injury to the kidnappers. The village warriors were unsuccessful in recapturing the women and shame hung like a dark cloud over the village for the past many decades.

The elders, of that early time, had had a ceremony lasting nine days to purify them from whatever misdeeds may have occurred causing the gods to allow such a degrading and shameful event to occur. All the men went into the sweathouses every night and sang songs to get the strength to combat such enemies and bring their women back. Since the women never returned, the village vowed to never permit such disgrace to fall upon them again and…it didn't.

Hatajah, one of the younger shaman leaders, suggested "The greatest honor for the Hidatsa would be to do something harmful to the white men from the north. Since the most well-known of them is the giant, would it not be likely that they would want to kill, injure or, at least, lay a hand or club on the giant?"

His remark was carefully considered and one by one, as the suggestion was mulled over by the wisest of the wise in the village, heads were nodded in agreement. Other suggestions were offered and considered but, since there was no war occurring at this time, they agreed an attack upon the giant was certainly one that would bring the greatest honor to an up and coming young buck.

The moccasin design and imprint was from a member of the same group of enemies that had raided them and stolen their squaws four and a half decades earlier. The memories were still sharp in the minds of the entire council. This would be an opportunity to show them that the Mandan have long memories and would not permit such activity to occur again without severe repercussions. The gentle smiley old men had turned into serious, scowling defenders of their tribe's lives and culture.

Plans were made to allow the night visitors to continue to observe them but without giving any indication of the Mandan having seen their well covered trails coming into the camp. Only a well-trained and sharp-eyed sentry had noted that a few uncovered tracks had appeared in sand that had been left smooth the evening before - just for the purpose of detecting snoopy neighbors from other tribes.

"I think he had other things on his mind," said the solemn faced sentry during his report to the council of elders. They agreed and said they were glad that the enemy had been so careless. In the dark, he hadn't seen the smoothed sand and had intended to brush out all of his tracks…but he'd missed a few!

Within a week, there was evidence of two more braves surveying the camp from the same location. Alert Mandan guards had been placed in the nearest lodges and they had been armed and watchful each night ever since the first warning was made by the moccasin tracks in the sand.

The elders correctly suspected that the greatest honor and reward would come to the enemy brave that actually touched or killed Kare. To lure the enemy to the center of their camp by using the simple minded giant, they were most eager to punish any interlopers.

A large empty V shaped space in the village was set aside to make the trap and all precautions were considered to catch the intruder but still protect the giant from harm.

"Consider the spider," said Torowa, the small, ancient, very dark and greatly loved shaman. "What can fly through its web without becoming entangled?"

"Nothing but a bird or a bat can pass through without capture, but insects and small creatures are immediately stopped. They are not seriously injured until it is the will of the spider. At the first hint of struggle, the spider races to the insect and wraps it tightly into a woven bag for its own reasons. Perhaps, we should just capture the hot-blooded boys and show them and their tribe that we have not forgotten the loss of our three women."

Torowa had been a warrior nearly half a century earlier when the abduction had occurred and the shame still smarted. One of the women had been an uncle's daughter and his family grieved for nearly five decades over the loss. Torowa became a peacemaker and his gentleness and kindness set the shining example for the entire tribe. His ability to solve disputes was used continually to prevent violence or anger within the community.

The location to be used for the trap would place the position of the spy's last observation point at the center of the widest part of the V shaped area with the point being the center of the village. The area would continue to be used during the day as usual. The giant would be positioned at the smallest part of the V in the center of the village so that it would be a large funnel pointing toward him.

Since the elders suspected that the emotions of enemy braves were clouding their better judgment, they wanted to make their enemies' entry into the camp appear unobstructed but their observations needed to be allowed without interference.

Within the V, all fires were intentionally made smaller and all children and women were moved to lodges deeper within the camp.

Immediately after sundown, several fine lines of tough buffalo hair and tanned leather string were stretched across the open space from the fire to the outer limit of the camp. The center fire was built slightly larger to illuminate the great man's favorite seat near the village pole, which was located in the center of the village.

Such a sight would make the temptation greater for the hot-bloods to want to strike. Each shelter had at least six alert Mandan warriors hiding inside to leap out fully armed with war-clubs and lances to capture the invaders. A few other tribe members moved about in the center of the camp but none between the invaders and the giant.

The greatly feared axe and sword of the huge man were absent and temptation was made to be irresistible! It was!

CHAPTER TWENTY-THREE

The Trap

The sun had been down for over an hour before the enemy invaders came creeping toward the Mandan camp. After the young Hidatsa men had determined the usual positions of the Mandan sentries on the higher knolls, three of them silently slipped through the low bushes and weeds toward their objective.

Their painted bodies perfectly matched the shadows and the movements they made were in absolute harmony with the breezes of the night. They would have been stepped upon before being seen, they were so well camouflaged. The self-confidence they felt easily overcame any fears or suspicions they should have had.

It was the chance of a lifetime they all desired and they kept total silence. The unarmed giant sat playing a dice game alone in the campfire light. His pets were taken into a lodge so they would not be apt to give any warning.

Throughout the camp, a few people left their sleeping areas for a final trip to the toilet before going to their blankets. Only an occasional person wandered anywhere near the soon-to-be victim's fire. The opportunity would never be better and communication by means of quiet finger taps on each other's bodies prepared the attackers to make the race to the giant and then return to claim their honors within their camp.

Just to touch him would get each of them an honor of an eagle feather to wear. To kill him would get them perhaps two feathers and be in legends for centuries to come. Each warrior carried a battle-axe and intended to use it on Kare, the biggest man that anyone had ever seen.

With their eyes set only on their victim, they slowly rose to a position to leap over the small bushes between them and their quarry. Simultaneously, they raced in nearly total silence as they approached the trap. Passing the outer lodges, they were in the center of the V when the toe of the moccasin on the leading attacker caught the first slightly raised string stretched across the path, causing him to land flat on his belly and slide in the sand. Almost immediately, the second attacker's foot snagged on another string causing him to dive headlong into the dust. The third attacker had passed the first two men when it was his turn to crash to the earth knocking the wind out of him.

The dust was still rising from the first man's stumble when the nearby shelters and lodges emptied of dozens of Mandan warriors racing toward the unwelcome fallen visitors. The first attacker to fall was lifting his arm to hurl a battle-axe when a Viking sword struck him on his throwing arm with the flat side of the blade, rendering it totally numb from shoulder to fingertip. Four to six men immediately covered his body with theirs causing him to be totally helpless.

The second man was on his knees when the shouting herd of Mandans landed upon him and his face was pressed so deeply into the dust of the camp that he had to be revived to prevent death. The Mandans had no desire to kill him but other, and better, plans had been drawn up and these plans were to be strictly observed.

The last attacker to fall was instantly surrounded by more men than could even reach to touch him through the human pack. Escape for the intruders, at that point was completely impossible!

Sentries on the other side of the camp had been tripled, as this could have been a ruse to get the attention of the Mandan to one side of the camp while the other side was being attacked. Since the three invaders hadn't shared their intentions with anyone of their own Hidatsa village for fear of being beaten to the prey, their camp, miles away, was peacefully sleeping.

Mandan scouts had been sent out to see if there were to be other points of invasion to the camp but it was not to be. The enemy camp was completely unaware of their would-be heroes plight.

The invaders were now captives and thoroughly tied with ropes around their ankles, wrists, waists and throats. The camp waited to see the attackers at a central fire, as did the entire council.

Lightening flashed nearby off to the west and a rainstorm was imminent. The council had the fate of the invaders planned before the raid even occurred. Two outcomes had been decided upon depending if any Mandan lives were lost.

Since no lives were lost among the Mandans, the lives of the attackers would be spared, but - with a powerful lesson for the enemies. This was to be a strong message to anyone ever causing injury to a Mandan again but an even stronger one showing that the white guests of the Mandans were sacred and to touch one inappropriately would be great reason for someone to suffer.

Torture was common among the all Skraelings and the young Hidatsa men had considered that risk as they'd planned the invasion. To them it seemed a risk worth taking.

The invaders were dumped unceremoniously on the opposite side of the fire from the council of leaders and shamen. The leaders merely looked upon the enemy as the equivalent of animal dung that was to be removed from the camp as soon as the unpleasant business was concluded.

An elderly Mandan tribal leader, once having been a Hidatsa slave who escaped, and had learned enough of the language for basic communication, began to speak. He informed the enemy prisoners of the punishment that would be forthcoming. Since their lives would be spared, it pleased the tribe to be as merciful as they could be.

In terms as brief as he could make them, he said, "Our hatred hasn't lessened since the stealing of the Mandan women nearly fifty winters past. The Mandan want to avoid war and have been patient, as long as there hasn't been any trespassing or stealing since that time. Now the line has been crossed and peace is being threatened as a result of your evil deeds.

"You three would be poor slaves as you seem to wish to live in ease and be treated as great warriors even though we are not at war. This council of Mandan leaders sees this punishment as suitable."

The elderly tribal leader continued, "We will keep all of your clothing and your weapons. We will give each of you two brands on your skin to remind you of your stupidity so you can tell others of your attempts to cause a war between our peoples. These brands will last as long as our sorrow has for our three stolen women.

"The first brand will be on your cheek and it is of a woman because you are more fit for woman's work than war. It will also be a reminder to your tribe of the women that were stolen from us when our elders were but young men. The second brand, on your buttocks, will be of a moccasin and it will be large to help you remember the mistake of attempting to offend our large guest."

Relieved that their lives were to be spared, the invaders felt their dread of death disappear. However, they were soon aware the mercy of the invaded camp was not as gentle as they had hoped.

Two long poles were produced and one was placed on either side of one captive. The captive was then tied to the poles at his feet, knees, waist and shoulders, and a tightly tied cap placed on his head and fastened to the poles totally immobilizing him.

A small smoking rock was removed from the hot fire with a pair of metal tongs provided by the Norsemen. The rock was chipped into a shape of a woman to be branded unto the cheek of each invader.

The captured Indian's fear was that the rock would fall into his eye and blind him so he made every attempt to hold perfectly still as the brand was being applied. It was held in place for several seconds before being taken back to the fire. A soft moan was heard as the trussed captive continued to feel the intense pain even after the rock had been removed. \

The camp observed with some surprise and even a bit of admiration as the intensely hot rock sunk into the flesh of the captive. Following that, he was flipped over from being face up to having his bare bottom exposed.

The next rock to be lifted from the fire was twice as long and wide as the average moccasin of the tribe's men. Its weight was such that a second man assisted the tong handler by placing heavy sticks at each end of the rock to lift it into position to place on the buttocks of the captive.

Smoke rose above the campfire as the flesh sizzled and, at that point the captive screamed so loudly that most of the Mandan camp jumped inadvertently. A large block of wood had been placed upon the rock to hold it in place for a moment. Following several seconds, the large rock was replaced in the fire to prepare it for its next use.

The odor of burning flesh covered the rows of spectators and the smoke and steam from the wound continued to rise for some moments following the removal of the rock.

The poles were removed from the first captive and placed next to another prisoner. The same punishment was administered to the other two members of the invasion party.

The Mandans were now satisfied that justice had been done and the lesson was concluded.

CHAPTER TWENTY-FOUR

Hidatsa Village

The three captives were untied and escorted by several Mandan warriors to the outer edge of the Hidatsa camp. The camp was many thousand strides from the Mandan campsite and it took them seven hours to make the trip.

The pain of the moccasin brand on their backsides prevented the enemy men from walking easily and they limped in pain while being prodded by Mandan men jeering and insulting them. Their burned buttocks were targets for the Mandan guard that frequently snapped leather whips or poked sharpened sticks at them to keep the downcast enemies moving rapidly. They felt the shame of not only being humiliated by being naked but also for yelling from the intense pain. Their bare feet were finding sharp twigs and rocks they would not normally have noticed in padded buffalo skin moccasins.

The Mandan men made sure the enemy camp was alerted to the return of the errant bucks and they remained at the outer edge of the camp to see that the branded men were noticed by the sentry. The Mandans then turned and returned the many miles back to their camp.

The reception in the Hidatsa camp was not what the invaders had anticipated. They were expecting to return as conquering heroes, not pathetic, naked specimens of an insulted enemy's wrath.

Walking as fast as they could, a difficult task to accomplish with extremely painful wounds on the buttocks and bloody feet, they made an attempt to reach their tents before the camp noticed them. The immediate yelling of the sentries, however, alerted every tent and many were able to witness the shameful reentry of the young men.

A Hidatsa council of leaders was immediately called to determine what should be done after such an event. The branded and bandaged men were called to explain their actions and why they weren't killed for such a stupid, impetuous act.

The scowling elders gazed upon the three renegade braves and remembered their own acts in years past and the repercussions of those events. One of the elders was an uncle of one of the bandaged men and was the first to speak.

"Nephew, my sister's son, why has this happened? Why have you come back to this camp in such disgrace? You cannot even sit as a man but have to kneel as a squaw tending a cooking pot. Your face carries burned messages of your foolishness. Do you forget that we haven't fought the Mandan during your lifetime, and even though we haven't been friends with them, we haven't killed each other?

"Did you forget that they have new allies with the white giants and with a man larger than any of us has ever seen? Do you forget the new medicines, weapons, foods and skills the Mandan now have? The giant alone can slice men in two parts with a single swing of his metal arm. Do you think that we should go to war with them?

"I do not like the Mandan just as our forefathers have never liked the Mandan, but to make war with them now is useless and foolish. We would all become slaves and wear brands as you do if we were even permitted to live. Our daughters and wives would be producing children for the Mandan while Hidatsa warrior bones bleach in a buffalo wallow or other shameful places they could force us to. Is that what you wish for your people, thoughtless puppy?"

Another elder added, "What can we do to prevent them from coming to our village and making war? Your actions showed them how weak we are, as we cannot retaliate for your mistakes without being butchered like buffalo. Our honor and strength is now small and they could defeat us anytime they wanted to with the white medicine and spirits helping them.

"You have brought unwanted attention upon us now and the white men of the north will help them since we didn't prove ourselves to be helpful to them as the Mandan did. We tried to kill them as they passed our nation and now we can expect them to exact revenge.

"Explain again the brands that they put on your bodies. Did you say that the brands on your cheeks were given to you because of the women we took from them when we were a much stronger people?

"Is there a manner of making a truce or peace with them where we could soften their anger and not worry about being exterminated with not a male left alive? This is a warning to our tribe that we are to be trod upon with a giant foot on our backs and we will not sleep comfortably again until we actively pursue peace with the Mandan."

A very tired appearing old man, wearing a ceremonial costume with skins and part of a buffalo skull on his head, looked up and all of the other members of the council immediately fell silent. The old man's trembling lips attempted to speak. He raised his hand and pointed a gnarled finger at each member of the group of elders.

Nawha, the owner of the ancient voice spoke.

"Fifty winters ago we were strong and bold. We took what we wanted and laughed at anyone that stood in our way. We laughed at the Mandan when they offered to smoke the white pipe to show we could live together on this land of many buffalo and deer. We took women from them when they proposed peace. Since then we found enemies in other tribes that had greater strength than we anticipated and that cost us greatly. We stole slaves from other tribes but they were sick with bloody coughs and we became sick, too, and many of our people died. Now we have done an act of war to a tribe that once desired our friendship and now could easily destroy us. Are we weak and foolish?

"Let us try to make amends with the Mandan and their white gods of the north so that we may live. Let us give them gifts and, if they accept them, give them back the women of the Mandan that have lived in our huts these many winters. This is my opinion."

A wave of shock went over the group of seated men. Give back women that had been wives for so many decades and mothers to their children? Was this the only solution?

Had it been any other man, the suggestion would be to go to the steam hut and seek wisdom from the steam and the use of medicines that give dreams. Every man in the council did that but…when they needed a solution to a problem immediately, they would ask Nawha. Nawha was nearing his one-hundredth winter and his whispers carried more weight than the bellowing of the strongest warrior.

Nawha pointed his bent finger at the three young men kneeling before them and said, " You have done nothing that these men sitting next to me in this council have not done in their day. Leave this fire wiser and repeat no mistakes."

As the three penitent men with the painful burning buttocks slowly shuffled out past the buffalo hide that was covering the entry, the rest of the council sat in total silence as they considered the verdict of the ancient one. In the time that Nawha had been on the council, their nation had not fought wars that depleted the young men and they no longer stole slaves from other tribes. It had been their longest period of peace ever.

When the white men had first approached them while returning from the forest with the Mandan, the Hidatsa had fired warning arrows to warn them off. The men told Nawha that the Mandan and white visitors had appeared unfriendly but now he had his doubts. These white men could have been helping this tribe as well as the Mandan if they had received a cordial greeting instead of arrows.

Later during the same week of the return of the three braves, a Mandan sentry's yell of alarm brought the village to life and the armed and alerted people stood in silence as two elderly women, dressed in the style of the Hidatsa, slowly approached the group.

Each of the old women had a small frame of poles that had wrapped bundles, such as would be used to travel while moving camps. It had been four days since the branded warriors had been sent back to their home village and the Mandan were still expecting some repercussions of that event. The Mandan elder that spoke the Hidatsa tongue was sent to meet them and ask what their business was because women of any group were generally protected.

The translator was shocked to hear Mandan being spoken back to him as he attempted to interrogate the elderly females. It was soon explained that these two ladies were captured as young women and had spent their entire lives since in the camps of the enemy. One had died but these two remained alive and now had been sent back to the Mandan nation with peace offerings from the tribe that had captured them.

The parents of both ladies were long dead and many of their siblings and cousins of their age had also already died. There were still several of their family members remaining, however, and a reunion was celebrated with a feast and a dance of gratitude and thanks.

The language of the Mandan, their childhood speech, seemed to have a different accent to the old women as they had rarely been able to use Mandan during the many years of captivity.

When the opportunity to speak to other captives presented itself, they were expected to speak only in the language of the captors so they wouldn't be so likely to make plans to escape or sabotage the Hidatsa camp in any way. Until they were trusted, no foreign speech had been allowed and, even after many decades of them living with the Hidatsa, speaking Mandan was discouraged.

The Norsemen took great interest in the event and thoroughly enjoyed the feasting and dancing. The former priest, Conn, wouldn't permit them to participate in the native dances because he felt that the religious nature of them would be offensive to the God which they, the Norse, worshipped. Conn did allow them to eat and drink with the natives and even permitted them to perform a Viking dance, which was accompanied by a flute and hand clapping.

The newly reunited former captives watched with great interest as the north men moved freely about in the camp and were so well accepted by the Mandan. In the Hidatsa camp, the rumors had been that the white men were cannibals. They also heard that they were magicians who could use evil magic to shrivel the limbs of their enemies and they could start fires by merely touching kindling. Many other stories had been told which the women could now see were produced by active imaginations accompanied by superstitions and folklore.

The Hidatsa tribe, as well as the Mandan, had believed that there was a white man in the group of their ancient gods and that he was a giant. Their stories of the origin of their people and land frequently commented on the giant white god and now…here he was! They had actually never seen a god or a giant before but here was actual proof - right before their eyes.

They observed the yellow hair and thick beards of the giants, the red-haired man that could get the other gods to kneel silently before him, the new foods, medicines and the weapons. Such beings were indeed gods and the Mandan had now befriended several of them.

CHAPTER TWENTY-FIVE

Return of the Slaves

It baffled the Mandan to see the largest white man to be the most humble. The giant tumbled and played with the tiniest children and they held him in great favor. He enjoyed stroking his pet bobcat, a wolf puppy and the little children, who swarmed around him constantly seeking his attention. He taught them silly little Norse songs and dances as well as several children's games that he remembered.

"What kind of a hero is this man? The adults admire him and the children adore him," thought the former captive women.

He had actually been seen splitting a grown man in half while in battle but now he was the first to console a crying child. When tears appeared in his eyes while holding a toddler that had just touched an ember in a cooking fire, the tribe was amazed.

The women recalled a Mandan legend about one of the founders of the Indian universe. The legend supposedly determined that a giant had been an original founder of all Indian nations and had lived during the creation of the world.

The giant, Kare, was mystified to see precious tobacco and corn pollen sprinkled in front of his lodge's entry each morning and wondered why only his shelter had been treated in such a way. He never asked and was totally unaware of the respect that he'd developed with the tribe. He had never been happier or more content than while playing with the children and his pets.

Torowa, the ancient elder, was still somewhat skeptical as he studied and carefully considered every action of the Norsemen. He was convinced they were only men and the new worship of the white men was possibly good for the tribe and the legends were frequently discussed and the moral strength of the group had increased. Torowa didn't make comments about the situation to any one. Besides, his daughter, Blossom, had married the red-haired shaman of the group.

The elderly female ex-captives soon became accustomed to the daily life in the Mandan village. Even though they were happy to be reunited with their few surviving friends and relatives, they were sorely missing their children, grandchildren and great-grandchildren back in the Hidatsa tribe's camp. They also missed their husbands of nearly fifty winters. They'd been known and loved and respected by the entire Hidatsa nation and they had come to think of it as home and themselves as Hidatsa. They were becoming very lonesome for the life back in the familiar village and wanted to return to their loved ones and old lodges.

The tribe couldn't understand why the old women would even think about wanting to return to that life after having been allowed to come back to the Mandan village. Hadn't they been grieving for almost fifty winters about their lost sisters and now the prayers had been granted since the white gods chose to dwell with the Mandan and gave them powers and blessings? The council was asked if the old women were possessed by the pagan magic of the other tribe or perhaps imposters to spy on the Mandan village? Many other thoughts were also brought up to the council.

Conn, the former priest, was allowed to sit in on the council meetings for this unusual problem dealing with the returned women. He was allowed even though he hadn't gone through the seven levels or lodges of the society to qualify him to sit with the senior elders. Blossom who was also a shaman, sat next to him.

Once Conn understood what the concern of the council was about, he simply said, "These ancient women are wives and mothers and grandmothers. Is it so wrong for them to miss those that they were allowed to bring into this life? Do not our own mothers give everything for our lives including their own, if required? Is not every Mandan mother willing to die several deaths for her children? So it is with mothers everywhere.

"These women are Mandan and you've seen how Mandan mothers give their lives for their families just as willingly as the bravest warriors and this is just as true with mothers everywhere. Could free passage back to the enemy camp be allowed so that they could spend their final years with the lives that they brought into this world?"

Conn continued, "Consider also the fact that many of the children born into the enemy Hidatsa camp are actually your sisters' children and therefore members of your own families and clans. They carry your family's expressions in their faces and share ancestors and clans with you. You have family members living there in the Hidatsa camp. Perhaps you would like and respect them if they lived in this camp."

Even though the translation was occasionally incorrect, Conn's use of the new language was increasing and improving rapidly. With Blossom's assistance, the elders attempted to consider every word and, after a lengthy amount of time, the comments of the former priest were understood. The hatred of the Hidatsa had lasted longer than the actual memories of anyone in either tribe and the feelings were greatly colored by unpleasant stories of massacres and scalpings remembered only by stories told them by great-great grandparents.

These events were alluded to and considered along with Conn's suggestions about allowing the old former captive women to go to the enemy camp again to see their families and then be given the choice of returning to the Mandan village or remain in the enemy's camp. Perhaps even allowing them to go back and forth between camps could be considered and then they could have an idea of the strength of this age-long threat.

Torowa, the beloved ancient elder, raised his head and waited a long minute before raising his hand to speak.

"I trust my sister (actually, his cousin) and the other woman," Torowa began. "These women have spent many summers and winters with the enemy against their wills but have now come to think of them as family too. They are good women and they would tell the enemy of our increased strength and blessings of the gods. Perhaps they would tell their children of our legends and family lore and thereby making them less a threat to the Mandan.

"The Hidatsa has not only given the women back to us but has sent gifts of sunflower, squash and bean seeds and tobacco. Would they have done that if they did not fear us and wish peace? The old women are now related to many of that tribe and would be a loss to that village if they were not returned. By allowing them to return, it shows that we are willing to negotiate and live in peace if we can.

"We could give the old sisters clothing of new buckskins in colors provided by our white guests that the enemy has never seen before and beads of glass sewn in front." Torowa continued. "Warm blankets of good wool and tightly knit would show our esteem for our old sisters. A white pipe for tobacco for their elder council may be a good idea too. We know that they are curious and interested in our white guests so we could perhaps offer the enemy an opportunity to send one of their tribe with the old sisters on their next visit. That may improve our strained relationship of many lifetimes. Maybe we could consider this."

Torowa lowered his hand to his lap and the council sat quietly out of respect for several minutes as they contemplated the old man's great wisdom.

While Torowa was supposed to be just another member of the council, his opinion carried enough weight to make events happen more quickly than if anyone else had said the same words.

It was decided that the ladies returning to the enemy camp would be given the choice of who to invite to come visit the Mandan camp and that the ladies would have the freedom to leave or reenter camp at their will.

The long, white clay pipe was unwrapped and filled with aromatic tobacco. After being lit from a glowing ember from the fire, it was passed from member to member.

All the members willingly smoked together showing that they were of one accord and the matter was settled.

CHAPTER TWENTY-SIX

The Return Home

Two days later, the village gathered together to properly see the elderly ladies leave for their familiar Hidatsa camp again. The common hope was that this parting would be short and a return trip would be occurring soon. Twelve young men of the tribe were to accompany them and the long poles that were commonly used to transport Indian belongings during trips were present.

Between them were blankets stretched so that the elderly women could sit on them as the men pulled them over the grassy slopes and around the lakes and hills. The ladies refrained from putting on the new finery until they approached the enemy village. Once within sight of the clearing in which the village stood, the escort of Mandans took all the luggage of the two ladies and placed it on smaller poles for them to transport into the Hidatsa village. The escorts then returned to their own homes.

The Hidatsa families of the captured Mandan women had been grieving as though the elderly women had died and been sent to their ancient homes with their tribes of birth.

To see them reenter the camp in rich finery and good spirits was almost beyond their comprehension and they danced with joy to have their beloved mothers and grandmothers returned to them. The entire village ran to meet them as they approached the camp.

Questions flew at them from all directions and it soon became obvious the long trip had exhausted the ladies and they were allowed to rest. Upon arising the crowd surrounded them again and demanded a total description of the adventure in detail.

The tribal council eventually rescued the returning heroines from the crowd and had them sit in council with the leaders of the Hidatsa tribe. The questioning continued but now it was interrupted with thoughtful pauses as the senior members digested each fact given to them with comments to each other before directing the discussion back to the women.

Nawha, the most elderly and respected shaman, offered a remark that everyone had been considering. Raising his trembling hand, he spoke. "Do enemies treat each other so? Haven't we offended the Mandan recently and then offered them the return of their sisters only to have them treat the women with great gentleness and return them to us with riches? I recall giving scalpless bodies back to enemies when I was a child. These people return our treasured women with even more treasure.

"Our thoughtless young men may have done us a tremendous service by attacking their camp in their stupidity so that we can now witness what a blessed nation the Mandan are. What sort of men guide the tribe with such wisdom that it makes us want to give them back even greater gifts than they give us without anger or malice toward them? Who are the leaders and shouldn't we find out what manner of direction they provide for that nation?"

A polite silence existed as the elders considered Nawha's remarks. It surprised the council when one of the returned women raised her hand to speak. It was unusual for anyone other than an elder to speak with out being requested to do so. The women had been allowed to speak earlier, but only to answer questions.

They solemnly nodded in permission to allow her to speak. She mentioned the offer of having a Hidatsa tribal member accompany them back to the Mandan camp to merely visit and meet the tribal council. She went on to remark that the senior shaman, Torowa, was the person to suggest this visit and he was known as being the man of greatest respect and honor.

The Hidatsa council listened with interest. They wanted to hear more about the members of the Mandan council but old Torowa seemed to interest them the most. It seemed as if his comments carried the most weight and were most respected. He was the Mandan to study. They also wanted to hear more about the white giants and if they indeed possessed godly qualities.

The women reported that the Norse had brought many new ideas with them and it appeared they were introducing them to the Mandan with good results. The fire starters that they used by simple chipping a flint against them to make sparks, the unusual clothing, the yellow flower medicines of the other world, their religion in which the red-haired man spoke and the white giants obeyed and other fascinating facts and stories that had been told to them by the Mandan tribal members during their visit to the camp.

The strange sharp weapons were discussed in detail as the women recalled them. Although they hadn't seen them in use, the tribal stories of how the Norsemen had attacked the forest people were retold daily and games for the children had been seen as each little boy wanted to be the berserkr that smote men in half with the sharp arm.

In addition to the gifts provided by the Mandan tribe, the white men had given them a piece of steel the women had mentioned. When struck against a hard rock such as flint, the steel would provide sparks for a fire. They had taught the women how to use this incredible invention.

What stories the ladies had to tell the elders and the clans of the Hidatsa that night at the fire. However, there was one thing they commented upon repeatedly to each other and that was how Nawha, the senior shaman of the Hidatsa looked so similar to Torowa, the senior shaman of the Mandan. They appeared almost identical, were of the same age range and even sounded alike. How could that be?

The questioning of the two old women continued for days on end. There had never been anyone able to describe the activities of a Mandan camp so thoroughly and with so many interesting characters as they had witnessed. Some stories were beginning to be questioned as to whether they were indeed true. Perhaps age had caused the elderly captors to imagine more than had actually occurred and some pursued that line of thinking. However, the women agreed on every point so that it would seem to be that they were speaking the truth.

Nawha, the senior Hidatsa shaman, was deeply troubled by a remark made by one of the women when she stated that he and the senior shaman of the Mandan, Torowa, looked so similar to each other. She went on to recall the several things that she'd noted such as appearance, wisdom, age, facial expressions and other traits that the two men had in common. She also commented upon the wide smile that both men usually wore during the day.

Nawha had been told that the only parents he knew had accepted him as an orphan into their lodge but he had no memory of any other parents. He'd only been told that his real parents were dead and that he was now living with parents that happily accepted him and he should never have any concerns about his past. But...now he did. Perhaps he should visit Torowa of the Mandan tribe and ask a few questions. Could there be a possibility of him having Mandan parents? Or was that other man a Hidatsa?

During the time of his birth, there had been many clashes with the other tribes of the plains. The taking of children and women was a common practice and the possibility existed that he'd been born into the enemy tribe. Had he hated his own people all these years?

In spite of his advanced years, Nawha decided to go with the women back to the Mandan camp to see this other man, Torowa, and talk with him about what could be their common ancestry.

The return trip occurred two weeks later. An escort of nearly twenty men pulled the crossed poles with the elderly occupants riding inside the three conveyances. Nawha was anxious to learn about the ancient shaman that lived in the Mandan camp and to see if they were related.

CHAPTER TWENTY-SEVEN

Nawha's Visit to the Mandan Village

The temporary camp of the Hidatsa escorts was placed on a hill nearby to the Mandan camp. It was six thousand strides (about one and a half miles) to the other village and both tribes seemed to feel comfortable with that distance.

While remaining alert, the small group of Hidatsa didn't feel particularly threatened by the much larger number of enemy so nearby. After all, hadn't they been invited to escort the Mandan women back to their original home with a Hidatsa guest? Since the gifts sent by the Mandan seemed generous and they could have treated the invaders of their camp much worse than they had, they didn't seem to be in a warring mood. In addition, they even allowed the captured women to return to the lives they had become used to and the families they had reared in the Hidatsa village.

The small Hidatsa group felt even more welcome when they found dried buffalo meat seasoned with fruits and berries left for them at the edge of their camp. Also, to make life easier for them, skins of freshly dipped well water from the big camp were placed close by so they didn't have to walk several miles to a river for drinking water.

The entire Mandan village stood quietly watching while the three elderly people in Hidatsa clothing approached them slowly. The twenty escorts remained at a considerable distance behind them.

The two former Hidatsa captive women assisted the ancient man walking between them. After stopping to rest at the edge of the lodges, they proceeded to the center of the camp where the council of elders was seated near the center pole of the camp.

The elderly trio approached to within three strides of the seated council before stopping. The two women remained next to Nawha to act as translators. Even though the two tribes did seem to have a few words of their languages in common, having the speech translated would be useful to both sides. The women were fluent in both languages and could translate more accurately than anyone else.

Blossom sat next to Conn, the former priest, and helped him understand the situation. His understanding of the Mandan language was improving daily but this situation was unique and he didn't want to miss anything.

As Nawha approached the seated council, he couldn't help but notice the tall bearded Norsemen standing amongst the tribal members. He recognized Kare, the giant, standing a head taller than anyone else in camp. The redheaded former priest also stood out from the darker skinned and black haired natives. However, the person that he most wanted to see closely was Torowa, the man that the former captive women had called the "Mandan Nawha."

The aged Hidatsa shaman raised both arms in a symbol of peace as he approached the council. Since there was no place to sit in front of the council, he would have to stand while giving his introductory remarks to them. Lowering one arm, he kept the other elevated in the common sign of wishing to speak. The council recognized it wordlessly.

The old man was dressed in his finest bleached buckskins and only modestly wore the three feathers in his hair of a senior chief in council. His moccasins were new and had beads of colored clay as decoration and he was an impressive sight as he stood before the group of leading men that had been enemies for his entire life and even long before. Torowa, his look-alike, sat in the center of the council, directly before him.

With his arm still elevated, Nawha began to speak. "Council of Mandans and white men of the far country. I come by your invitation to see you today and to address three issues that we of the Hidatsa tribe feel to be important to us. My tribe's council has approved of the first two issues and asked me to bring these thoughts to you."

The entire camp was silent except for a crying baby and a pet coyote puppy that was chasing an annoying rodent of some sort between the lodges.

The old man's words were not as loud as might be expected from a younger man and everyone wanted to hear the original words, which they didn't understand, as well as the women's' translation.

Nawha's remarks continued. "It is the wish of the entire Hidatsa council to thank you for your treatment of our young men who so thoughtlessly invaded your camp to count coup on the white giant. We found your punishment to be not only merciful and appropriate for such an ill plotted disgrace but also informative. Had they committed such an insult to any other tribe or, had it been done to Hidatsa, they would now be dead men rather than chastised youth just beginning a useful life. None of the other men of our nation are apt to ever attempt such a stupid feat again. The Hidatsa nation apologizes for that act.

"Having three of your women as captive had nearly faded from our thoughts after fifty winters have passed," Nawha continued. " We think of them as Hidatsa and have overlooked the pain and shame of your loss. It was our hope that the return of these women would express our shame of the attack of the young men upon your camp but now the loss would be felt by many Hidatsa as these women are now the wives, mothers, grand mothers and loved by the entire camp. One Mandan woman did die many seasons past but we reluctantly willed to return the surviving two to their original homes here in the Mandan nation.

"The hundreds of relatives of these women in our village were saddened greatly to have to release these women to come back here to what could be only strangers to them now."

The council sat expressionless as the translators attempted to repeat each phrase as clearly as possible and frequently compared their interpretations to determine just the right meaning. Nawha stood with his arm still elevated but it was shaking a little by now.

Nawha wet his lips with his tongue and with a voice that had lost some of its volume, began again. "We hoped that the return of these stolen women would show our gratitude toward your kindness.

"However, the second reason for my coming here to thank the Mandan nation was for the return of these women again to their adopted home with us in the Hidatsa camp. We had performed dances and prayers for the dead as they left us. Their husbands, children and children's children grieved for the loss of two beloved tribal members at one time. They had become loved by all and we all deeply grieved as they watched the women walk out of camp to return here"

The old arm sank somewhat and his voice became so soft that even the translators moved closer to hear what he was telling the council.

Nawha continued. "I cannot tell you the joy that our nation felt as we saw the beautifully dressed and smiling ladies enter our camp after returning from here. We feasted and had dances for days in thanks for the return of the dead. Their families gave gifts to everyone. Such events have only occurred a few times in my long life such as when the buffalo came back or rains came to end a parched summer.

"That is the second reason for coming here today. The council wants to thank the Mandan Nation for allowing these women to return to their adopted homes with us and to their families that cherish them above all things.

The Mandan nation has proved repeatedly that you deserve to be great and for the generous acts you perform, you deserve to be blessed above all nations. That is my opinion."

CHAPTER TWENTY-EIGHT

The Brothers Finally Meet

The elderly Hidatsa shaman's raised arm was tiring as he stood before the somber Mandan council. His legs were tiring and he felt his voice beginning to tremble as he approached his third reason for coming to address his ancient enemies.

Torowa would have summoned a tribal member to bring a seat for the aged guest but that would mean interrupting him while he was speaking and that was unacceptably rude. A man with his arm raised was to be given total attention until he lowered his arm of his own accord.

It seemed that the standing old man was reaching the end of his opening remarks and Torowa noticed him swaying as he spoke.

Standing but deeply bent over, Torowa lifted his own heavy stool and bent nearly double so as not to have his head higher than the speaker, carried his stool to the ancient Hidatsa and placed it behind him. He then, remaining deeply stooped, returned to his place at the center of the council and sat, cross-legged, in his normal place. Every face remained expressionless and no one displayed emotion in any manner.

Gratefully, the aged Hidatsa slowly lowered his body to sit on the leather-covered stool and continued to speak as if no interruption had occurred.

Both Hidatsa and Mandan manners would have prohibited this indication of lack of attention during such an important matter but this situation was unique in many ways and this informality wasn't to be taken too seriously. The speech wasn't actually interrupted and the falling over of the speaker would have been both an embarrassment to him as well as unprofessional.

With his voice regaining strength, Nawha continued. "I mentioned that I had three reasons for desiring to visit this Mandan village. The third is not one of interest to anyone other than Torowa and myself. I would prefer to discuss this with him in privacy with only our interpreters present, if this can be arranged."

Nawha was incorrect in saying that the subject should be of no interest to anyone other than the two senior shamen. The entire village wanted to know the business of every other person and the events of today would be discussed in great detail for decades to come. That would include the private meeting of Torowa and Nawha.

Nawha knew Indians intimately and whatever was discussed between the two of them would be of enormous concern to everyone in both villages. However, he would let Torowa give out as much information of their private conversation as he chose to in his own good time.

Members of the Mandan council spoke in turn following Nawha's remarks and display of gratitude. When it came to Torowa's time to speak, he didn't remark on the resemblance they had to each other but rather commented on how events that had occurred recently had led to a positive outcome and he hoped a favorable relationship between the tribes might continue. He suggested that the aged shaman rest for sometime in his personal lodge and they could have their visit after resting. Nawha and the ladies were then given food and drink before resting for the remainder of the afternoon.

Properly rested and feeling ready to talk about matters that were perhaps more personal, Torowa, Nawha and the two women sat at a small fire near the center of the camp but with everyone notified that privacy was requested for this meeting.

Nawha began. "It interested me when these ladies returned to our camp with news that another man is almost as ugly as I am. I couldn't believe that so I had to come and see for myself."

Torowa brightened. This was the kind of conversation that he enjoyed the most with lots of hidden insults and humor. He'd certainly never expected to have the opportunity to be talking to a Hidatsa in this manner but perhaps this old man could amuse him and something else could come of this meeting too.

He replied to Nawha, "Now you will see yourself as pretty having met me, I suppose."

"When someone like myself has so little to be proud of, ugliness gives me a special place in the world and I don't wish to compete for it." was Nawha's reply.

Torowa responded by saying, "I've always said that I'd give my best moccasins to someone who looked worse that me but you won't be wearing them soon. You have to get much homelier to qualify for my skins."

Each man knew their own reflection well enough to realize that they were looking at themselves when they looked at the other man. They were nearly identical!

Torowa knew that he'd once had a twin brother. His mother had been picking berries one day when a party of Hidatsa hunters had surprised her. Carrying her twin sons, she'd found a berry patch at a lengthy distance from the village. The enemy warriors saw her and hid in the low brush to secretly approach her. She had attempted to outrun them while carrying the two baby boys but an arrow had been shot to attempt to slow her down by wounding her.

The arrow had penetrated the blankets and carrying pack in which one boy was carried and it appeared to have deeply penetrated his tiny chest. Carrying two packs hampered her running, each pack containing one son. Her only hope of escape was to take the uninjured one and outrun the enemy warriors into camp, which was still a considerable distance away.

Carrying the pack with the uninjured child, she raced screaming into the camp warning every one of the enemy hunters chasing her.

Returning to the berry patch slightly later, with a large group of armed warriors to look for the injured infant, the sad mother met only disappointment. She found a very bloody baby blanket where she'd been picking berries - but no baby. The disappearance of the child had been a mystery in the Mandan camps for decades.

Torowa, could remember hearing of the incident as a child, from his parents. Nawha had wanted to ask Torowa about his birth and was very interested in this story.

At its conclusion, Nawha, wordlessly and slowly opened the front of his garment and a deep jagged scar from an ancient wound crossed his chest.

"I think that we are brothers," Nawha said. "This scar was on my chest from a time before I had memory."

With a large tear rolling down his cheek for the first and only time in his adult life, he said softly. "Tell me about our parents and our other family."

The translator's eyes were glowing with tears as they realized that the greatly loved and respected chief and shaman of the Hidatsa tribe was truly a Mandan – just as they were!

CHAPTER TWENTY-NINE

Sir Paul's Search

Sir Paul Knutson often wondered what had become of Bjoro, Father Pettersson and the rest of the crew that had gone to the far off new world to look for the missing Greenlanders. It had been two years since the knorr had returned from the great inland sea with only a few hands aboard. The remaining crew had reported that the riverboat had not returned to the inland sea, as it had been assigned to do. With winter rapidly approaching, the remaining crew reluctantly departed without them.

It wasn't a rare event to lose a ship and crew but Sir Paul always felt that this group would come back successfully. He was confident they had gotten to the interior of that strange country and were still there awaiting Norse sails to bring them home. He had developed enormous confidence in this particular crew, as they seemed to possess an abundance of every skill required for an exploring expedition.

Sir Paul had become a very wealthy man since leaving the sailing to others and was now enjoying the trading business with his wines and beers selling well everywhere. He was considering the prospect of leaving Norway to settle in the French grape growing country so he could be close to what he loved the best. Margret liked the warmer climates and would happily move there, too.

Sir Paul felt somewhat responsible, however, for the ship and crew that he had arranged a few years earlier. His companies now included many ships, vineyards and wineries and money was coming in faster than he could spend it.

The Crown was having financial trouble and the chances of getting another crew to cross the North Sea was becoming less likely if they had to depend upon the King's generosity.

Considering what could be done to send a ship or two to the great inland sea (Hudson Bay) and to the same area where the riverboat was sent off, Sir Paul carefully counted the cost and began to look at the possibilities.

The assistant captain of the second journey's returning ship was still sailing, but now as a full captain. Sir Paul thought perhaps he could convince this captain to take another trip to the same area to see if Bjoro or any of the others had returned there. Riverboats could be towed across in the same manner as they were on the first inland trip. Now a newer weapon was available in case the Skraelings became a nuisance. Crossbows!

All the sailors could easily be trained to operate the deadly weapons and thereby outshoot the Skraelings' weaker long bows. Those long bows had caused problems in the past as the enemy were usually better shots and used to the terrain. Some countries considered the new crossbows to be uncivilized weapons that should not be used by Christian men. However, crossbows could give the Norse a considerably better chance against the Skraelings!

In addition, an explosive Chinese concoction had been brought to Europe and the possibilities were interesting. By igniting this black powder, an explosion was created and it could propel a rock or piece of metal a substantial distance when it was all packed into a hard tube or a pipe.

Sir Paul silently wished the red-haired priest were here, as this sort of thing would fascinate him. The curious little fellow continually used his magnifying glass to study everything around him and his conclusions were fascinating to anyone with an interest in their surroundings.

"The most curious man I ever met and probably the most intelligent," thought Sir Paul. "His advice would be very helpful with this experiment."

Metal pipes worked best, concluded Sir Paul, after seeing a clay pipe explode during an experiment on his winery grounds. One of his men was slightly injured as a heavy piece of clay flew high in the air and struck him even though he'd stepped behind a barricade after lighting the fuse.

Hundreds of trials proved that carefully measured amounts of the black powder packed into the tube with either a solid metal pellet, rock or a handful of small rocks could be ignited and cause the rocks or pellets to deliver a deadly load.

Targets were installed at varying distances and sights for guiding the shot were set on the tube to help them point the tube for maximum destruction. The loud explosion would sound like thunder and could be heard for great distances. Fire and smoke accompanied the discharge and the crew and bystanders found this to be highly entertaining.

This could possibly be a useful weapon if it were more portable as it was heavier than a man could easily carry for any distance. Perhaps such a device could be mounted on the riverboats to scare off Skraelings since actually hitting one could be difficult and even unlikely.

Sir Paul set to work immediately to find the crews and ships. He had little trouble finding the same captain of the previous expedition who had waited for the returning river explorers on the great inland sea. The captain said he would be willing to return to that inland sea docking place for the substantial sum that Sir Paul was willing to pay him. He also would hire a fighting crew with additional training on the deadly crossbows and "noisy pipe" as it was commonly called.

Recalling the Black Plague caused such damage on his first voyage to the new world, Sir Paul used the same techniques to prevent rats from entering the ship for this trip. This lesson of rat removal and hygiene had not been wasted on Sir Paul but most of the world ignored such an unlikely remedy.

Father Pettersson had been very strict about the elimination of vermin and that seemed to have worked well. This same captain had been on that trip as an assistant to Bjoro and knew the effectiveness of the young priest's sanitation methods. Without fully knowing the reason for the good results, he knew sanitation seemed to be useful and did attempt to use that knowledge.

Sir Paul had mounting racks built on the bow and stern of the riverboats so that the explosive pipes could be solidly attached and wouldn't bounce themselves over the opposite gunwale when fired. Each weapon, when aimed, could be pivoted one hundred and eighty degrees on heavy metal swivels, so that the entire boat wouldn't have to change course in order to fire.

Using an uninhabited wooded shoreline, targets were set up to test the new weaponry upon imaginary enemies. It pleased Sir Paul and the crew to see how effectively their shooting pipes and crossbows performed. The results of the tests were astounding! Never had man had such power to defend himself - or attack others. The powerful crossbows sunk a fired bolt twice as deeply as a long bow and at a much greater distance with greater accuracy. In addition, the firing pipes could drive a heavy metal ball or a handful of rocks into trees causing enormous damage.

Even though trading was a far better profession than war to Sir Paul, he had been an excellent warrior on occasion and the art of battle was a part of his heritage. Many of his Viking ancestors would have been delighted to have the devices he now possessed, to wreak havoc upon the poorly defended foreigners.

Nothing had been imagined to compare with these contrivances. A fleeting thought was that such fighting machinery could be satanically inspired, but Sir Paul soon reconsidered that thought and accepted it as a gift from God to defend His Christian kingdoms.

Satisfied that the ships were properly fitted out and prepared for the voyage, Sir Paul requested that Nicholas of Flynn, his old friend and navigator, ask the parting blessing on this voyage with hopes that they would again make contact with the missing Norsemen of the second journey.

This trip began in 1364.

CHAPTER THIRTY

Red Haired Twins

Two winters had passed since the Norsemen had moved far to the west with the friendly Mandan tribe. The association proved to be beneficial to both groups and, while the newness had worn off, they were still treated as welcome guests and allowed all the privileges of tribal members.

Relations with the nearby Hidatsa had improved greatly since their beloved Nawha had been identified as a twin brother to the great Mandan leader, Torowa.

Both tribes had very strict rules regarding marrying within clans and now the tribes realized they had several members of the same clans. A serious study of who could marry each other was taken so that no one of a clan of either tribe could consider marriage with another member of the same clan.

Elderly ladies of the two tribes with good memories were given the responsibility of keeping a record of the clans and they took this job very seriously. This was complicated even within one tribe and now there were two tribes. They found they weren't familiar with each other to the degree of knowing who was in which particular clan.

Happily, however, the choice of mates was greatly increased with two tribes to choose from under the new peace conditions.

Nawha had taken the allowed four wives and had fathered twenty-one children. When he attempted to count his offspring, grandchildren and great-grandchildren, the number came to well over one hundred and twenty tribal members that had considered themselves to be full blooded Hidatsa but now were found to be also quite closely related to the Mandans.

Beyond that, Nawha learned that he was a cousin to one of the captive women that had been stolen half a century earlier. When the children of the captive women were considered, over three hundred Hidatsa members had Mandan blood.

When these facts were mentioned at a tribal council, the question was raised, "How can we be angry with the Mandan if so many of our tribe share that same blood?"

While Nawha felt he had answers to that, it seemed best that he wait and see what the other council members had to say first.

Two other younger council members were descendents of his and thereby of Mandan descent too. They were somewhat uncomfortable as the question was discussed.

In an attempt to lighten the situation, another elder shaman remarked.

"There will be no more women taken from the Mandan as they could be our cousins and clan members and we shouldn't risk our lives to steal a wife for another man."

Since there hadn't been a woman raid for fifty years, that did not really fit reality but it did relieve the tension enough for others to speak.

Nawha knew that no member would say anything to offend him as the cherished ancient chief, so he looked around and slowly raised his hand to speak.

"Hidatsa chiefs and brothers, may I speak?" asked Nawha.

A slow moment passed as he sat quietly with his hand in the air. The council was totally quiet, as they knew his feelings would become tribal policy as they had been for some several past years.

"As you know, I have been a faithful Hidatsa chief and shaman for more winters than some of you are old," Nawha began. "I have never allowed any action of this tribe to occur that would cause harm in any way to it, without much lengthy thought and serious discussion. I have fasted for many days and steamed my body to get my mind focused correctly on problems so that this nation would not be lead in the wrong direction, causing harm to it. Many dances were called to help make decisions and I have willingly tortured my body for the well being of the Hidatsa tribe. All the levels of leadership are a part of my past and I am now given honor as a senior chief and shaman.

"It is with total humility when I say that on those occasions when I was overruled, this tribe stumbled and suffered."

The council remembered in shame that this was the truth and how they had made some incorrect decisions that had proven exceedingly costly when Nawha's advice had not been taken.

The small, dark, ancient man continued.

"I am but a man and not superior to anyone. I have no guidance from our creator beings to tell me when something is apt to go awry or if it may profit us. The movement of the buffalo isn't given to me in a dream or by much steam or smoke. It is by studying the heavens that I can forecast the weather but not from knowledge provided by gifts of the gods.

"It may be to my credit, if you wish to admit it, that we have enjoyed a long period of peace with the Mandans. It has long been my policy to display gentleness to each other and to those that could benefit us by being peaceful. It would be to our Hidatsa nation's benefit to send shamen to learn the Mandan tongue and determine how the tribes are separated into clans. Intermarriage is not acceptable unless the man and woman are of separate clans be they of Hidatsa or Mandan tribes. We already share blood and to mix it improperly would bring a heavy curse to both nations.

"We have our two greatly loved and respected women that had been born in the Mandan nation but now live in ours. They can help us learn the language and also determine how our clans have formed so that the births of future children will not be of the parents who could be related and in the same clan. Such unions of mixed clans are unacceptable to both nations. I have thought about this and believe it to be important to us. These are my opinions."

Conn remembered fondly the peculiar courtship that he and Blossom had enjoyed.

She'd been his teacher of the Mandan language and he had shown her the astounding world of the tiny creatures with his magnifying glass. They had compared the strange swirling skin on the ends of their fingers, peered at the many different types of hair they could find, dissected insects and fish as well as leaves and soil. Other members of the tribe were frequently nearby but Blossom's father also found much pleasure in the new knowledge. The red-haired man greatly amused him as well as interested him.

Conn and Blossom had spent hundreds of hours discussing, studying, comparing, arguing and laughing at the incredible numbers of interesting phenomenon surrounding them. They frequently had Torowa, and now often Nawha, deeply involved and found the elderly men's intelligence to be far beyond what would be suspected by just appearances.

Conn had described some of the newer Italian schools that allowed any type of question to be asked and the amazing answers that had come from such places. He had also shown them how information could be permanently recorded in the written word, replacing their pictographs, so it could be referred back to for generations.

Blossom and Torowa had shown him wonders of nature that he realized could possibly be harnessed into useful features of their lives.

The Mandan belief that all plants had some use for healing made sense to the former priest and he was delighted to learn that the inner bark of the willow tree was a fine pain reliever. Conn decided he would keep parcel of it nearby for the rest of his life. The Mandans were equally as happy to have received the miraculous dandelion from the Norsemen and the remarkable medicine that it provided.

This wonderful knowledge was all about him and he now had someone of curiosity and intellect to share it with him. He remembered how some monks had attempted to convince him that all useful knowledge had already been given to them and there was no need to seek any more.

"How incredibly sad to think in such narrow terms," thought Conn. Blossom, her father and uncle were all of the same mind as Conn.

He hadn't been oblivious to the beautiful Blossom at his side. He looked at her … a lot! She was indeed a delight to look at as well as to talk to and laugh with. She became the redheaded Conn's best friend and confidant. They became inseparable and when she was out of sight, for even a few moments, he became uncomfortable.

The former priest didn't know how to conduct his own marriage ceremony - but to live with Blossom, without God's permission, wasn't acceptable. Even though he had no one to discuss this with from the church, he'd seen enough of other priest's unacceptable relationships with women back in Europe to realize that this situation would have to be decided by him and him alone. He would forever remain a man under God's authority!

He had asked Blossom to become his wife and not merely his woman. She appeared to fully understand what he meant but the situation concerned her, as she knew he was a man who was not to have a relationship with a woman while he wore the black robe. He was a man that was sincere and of great character so what would he do? What could he do?

Conn had always known well the results of fasting and prayer and that became his course of action. When he'd first considered marrying Blossom, he left the camp and walked to a knoll a few miles away and, for three days, that small hill was his chapel and he fervently prayed. He didn't sleep, touch food or drink for the entire time.

Wearing his hooded black robe, the priest knelt in the heat of three days sun in constant prayer and fasting. He didn't allow a drop of water to touch his lips during the entire time.

At the end of that time of soul searching, the young priest raised to his feet with difficulty and stumbled back toward the camp, falling on several occasions with a large audience of Mandan silently standing at the outer limits of the village observing, with great concern, the return of this small leader of the Norsemen.

None had greater concern than the beautiful Blossom, who was carrying a skin and gourd of water to give her dearest friend a drink the moment that he stepped across the outer village limit. This was according to the ancient custom that the person must reenter the camp unassisted.

As was the Mandan custom, the women were bare breasted during the greatest heat of the day and Conn saw her through the eyes of a man suffering from dehydration and exhaustion as he stumbled to his knees in the final twenty steps from the camp. Arising, his eyes met hers and the final hurdle of his test was cleared. His thought was, "If I had ten lives to live, I'd happily give my life for this woman every time." His decision had been made!

Entering the sweathouse, the former priest felt that his prayers had been answered and this act of bathing only cleansed his body as he felt that his soul had been purified upon the knoll in the past days.

A concerned and attentive Blossom stood by as he left the sweathouse and together they approached her father's lodge. She'd watched him unnoticed from a nearby patch of willows as he'd attempted to seek guidance in this troubling matter.

She softly asked, "Conn, did you receive knowledge these last days that would allow us to be married in a manner that pleases your God?"

Squeezing her hand, he lifted it to his lips, and replied, "My God gave me strength and wisdom in my beliefs long before I met you. Now I have a much clearer picture of what is to be my course in life and living with you will not be counted as a sin but rather as a sanctified act that makes us man and wife with an obligation to have children. We will have a ceremony that I will officiate at as God's chosen representative here and this must be carefully explained to you so that you agree. We will discuss this situation with Torowa and ask his approval. If both of you agree to these terms, we can be married soon. Very, very soon!" He said as he gently kissed her hand, one finger at a time.

Smiling broadly, Blossom threw her arms about Conn's neck and kissed him repeatedly. He then knew that she would have agreed to the marriage terms without even listening to them! He was totally exhausted but having her this close reminded him that marrying this woman was now his greatest desire!

Less than a year later, in the Mandan camp, Torowa, the tiny senior chief, looked with amazement upon the newly born red-haired twin boys held in the arms of his smiling daughter, Blossom.

Conn stood by with a huge smile of happiness on his face while gazing lovingly upon the three most important people in his life. He had capably assisted the experienced midwife in the delivery and the births had gone well. The surprise of having twins had overwhelmed them all.

Smiling broadly and sitting next to him was Torowa, the grandfather, who had also been a twin. So, this was fitting, but totally unexpected.

All the other Norsemen had taken Mandan wives and several of them already had children.

The only one not married was Kare, the giant. Kare had neither the desire nor ability to have a wife or children even though he was always ready to care for the babies of others and was usually seen with several little ones at his feet playing with him.

His pets included a bobcat, a coyote and an orphaned buffalo calf. His pet crow stole items from everyone in the village but, being it was Kare's, it was tolerated and even accepted. All of these creatures filled his life!

His reputation as a berserkr would last centuries after his death but he was never again called upon to perform the act that got him the title of "The man that can cut a man in half". He never thought of it after living with the Mandan.

Shorthorn, now known as Ivar, was nineteen and asked Conn about having more than one wife as four were permitted by the tribe. The furrowed brows and scowling countenance of the former priest should have told him the answer but it wasn't until Conn had given him a number of good reasons why it would be best not to marry multiple times that Ivar reconsidered.

Ivar had gotten to know several young ladies he would have liked to have in his harem, but Father Carrots still held the reins with the Norsemen.

CHAPTER THIRTY-ONE

The Search for the Missing Crew

Following a rather uneventful ocean crossing and reentering the big inland sea of the north, Sir Paul's expedition docked at the mouth of the river in the same spot on the great inland sea where they had been two years earlier. No signs existed of anyone having been there since their leaving the place at that time.

As on the trip before, ten men were to remain at the ship while twenty others took to the river. Using the bored out mooring stones as a guide, they followed the water south. Shooting pipes were mounted on the smaller riverboats as the chance of meeting enemy Skraelings in battle was greatly increased on rivers and lakes.

It was a few weeks later that the party saw the mooring stone with the white circle on it that Ivar had made at Bjoro's request. The crew carefully examined the nearby campsites. Close scrutiny indicated there had not been any apparent urgency about leaving this site so they traveled onward continuing to study the banks as they went.

Keeping their crossbows at the ready and the shooting pipes prepared for action, the Norsemen walked onto some of the banks looking for evidence of their countrymen having been there. A rather promising looking site kept them occupied for hours, looking it over to determine as to whether or not someone had camped there in the recent years.

Signs of the Skraeling abounded and the Norsemen had no desire to have an altercation with them. Sagas about the stealth and cunning of the brown enemy had circulated the decks of ships and inns for centuries already and the sagas usually had the Skraelings winning the battles and the Norsemen running for their lives.

A particularly pleasant looking site with a fine docking area appeared and the small river craft cautiously slipped up to it. No mooring stone was available but they had seen one only an hour back.

The crew felt if anyone had been here, they may have felt so secure they didn't feel the need to bore a mooring hole. Actually, there really was not a decent boulder right on the site so they could have tied up to a branch if they had indeed been here two years earlier.

Slipping up to the comfortable looking site, they commented upon how this would have been a better place to tie up than the one with the white circle they had passed earlier in the day.

A small smoldering pot of embers, to light fuses, stood near each of the shooting tubes and the crossbow men stood behind their shields at each approach as the Skraelings were sure to know the Norsemen were here again.

Two unarmed men leapt from the craft to shore and darted around what had been the last camp of the Norsemen two years earlier. What had to have been graves were found but the number of men within was unknown. The graves had been disturbed and human bones were scattered nearby.

A large gray rectangle of granite type rock was lying on the ground near the gravesite. The men, both of which were unable to read the writing, called to the ship saying they had found an engraved stone.

Lifting the heavy rock, together they carried it close to the ship for interpretation. The captain's first mate climbed down from the ship to look at the stone. He read the message and copied it unto a piece of tanned leather. While he was studying the stone an arrow, making a sizzling sound, ricocheted off the rock in front of him.

The three men ashore dove into the river craft leaving the gray stone on the shore. Sliding behind the large shields as several more arrows thudded into the side of the craft, the men prepared to fight back.

The men at the shooting pipes had wanted to try their new invention and this was the opportunity they had been eagerly awaiting.

Taking burning sticks from the smoldering ember pots, they touched the saturated wick that led into the pipe and the combustible powder. Within a second, rocks and pebbles that had been stuffed down the barrel exploded into the trees where the Skraelings had hidden.

The wide pattern of the shot splattered several yards of trees and brush and struck several of the Indians hiding in the leaves. Leaves and limbs off the trees fell like rain for a moment.

The thunderous noise, the flames and the burst of smoke startled the natives so that they raced back into the forest to consider what had just occurred here to them.

"How have the white invaders captured thunder, lightning and clouds into their boats to hurl at us?"

"What sorts of gods protect these men that they have such powers?"

"What can we do to chase them off when they can deliver magical evil upon us?"

Seeing the boat leave shore, the seventy Skraelings waited until they were slightly out of longbow range to approach the bank of the river for a closer look at the "Thunder Boat." It was there they discovered the range of the crossbow as the speeding short bolts penetrated their ranks killing two warriors outright and wounding several others. Another blast of the firing pipes had the natives crashing through the woods in total panic.

The assistant captain wrote several messages on tanned beaver skins so the rock carvers would have the correct words to tap into the stones they were going to leave behind.

One stone had this message chipped into it:

JOURNEY FINANCED BY SIR PAUL KNUTSON TO LOCATE CREW OF 1362
BELIVE TO BE ALL DED FROM SKRAELINGS
FOUND BOAT TO BE BURNED AND SUNK
MAY GOD REMEMBER THEM 1364

The second stone had these words on it:

SIR PAUL WILL SEND A SHIP EVERY TWO YEARS TO NORTH INLAND SEA FOR SIX MORE YEARS IF A SURVIVOR SHOULD FIND THIS GO THERE TO MEET IT   1364

The third stone said this:

LEAVE A CARVED STONE AT INLAND SEA TELLING US WHERE TO FIND YOU IF YOU CANNOT STAY THERE WE WILL BE BACK   1364

These stones were hurriedly chipped out, as the boat was several hundred yards off shore and out of arrow range. They were then thrown on shore near the burned out boat of the first expedition, whose mast and bow ornament still stood above the water.

They thought perhaps the missing men would return to that place if they were expecting another group to rescue them.

CHAPTER THIRTY-TWO

Conclusion

Over the many years the Norsemen spent with the Mandan, several more stones were carved describing the numerous events and other interesting situations that had occurred to them and the tribe. They never saw another white man during their lives.

When the last Norseman died in 1411, their tearful children and grandchildren brought all the carved stones into one lodge of honor. For many generations, whenever the death of a Norseman was mentioned in a story, it was mentioned "even the dogs wept" at their loss. The skulls of the white men were placed in a circle around the lodge and the tribal members often visited the skulls to talk to them and tell them the latest gossip and jokes.

The bodies were treated just as the Mandan dead were. After grieving, the Mandan placed the dead Norsemen upon scaffolds a good distance from the camp for several months. After decomposition had done its job, all the bones were collected and buried except for the skull.

The skull was then brought back to the village and placed in a circle outside the village proper. The skulls of the northern guests were larger than the typical Indian's but the largest of all was that of Kare, the Giant. A small offering of pollens and healing herbs were placed before his enormous skull by a loving group of natives that had been cared for as infants and children by the gentle giant.

The Norsemen were treated as gods even though the tribe knew them to be as human as they themselves were. It was always good to let the other tribes be aware of how the Mandan were treated by gods to the degree that the immortal beings even came to live with them.

The skull of Torowa, the long dead beloved elder, seemed to be smiling wider in death than he even did in life! The teeth of all these men were given to the families of the village and then placed in treasured "medicine bundles" to be used for prayer and to accompany the Mandan to special dances and meetings.

Norse ships had returned to the new lands twice in the following years looking for possible survivors but after the second trip, they felt it was a lost cause.

Five hundred years later, in 1917, another Swedish farmer was plowing a level part of his farm on what had once been a shoreline of a large lake. As he plowed, he hit a large gray rock and soon came across two more. To his astonishment, there was ancient writing upon all three of them.

He knew of and recalled all too well the disgrace and abuse Olof Ohman had suffered after discovering the stone, which had caused so much ruckus.

Having no desire to have that happen to him and his family, the farmer hitched his team to a hay wagon and placed the three stones he had just found in the bed of the wagon. The stones weighed about three hundred and twenty pounds all together.

He then drove the several miles to the site of the original stone.

He had never met Ohman or Nils Flaaten, Ohman's neighbor, who had also been accused of contributing to the hoax. Nils was having coffee with Olof when the stranger drove the team and hay wagon into his yard. When the two men heard of the discovery by the neighbor and saw the stones, they both recalled the past eighteen years of shame and accusations.

Both men answered together and the farmer heard them say, "Bury the damned things! Don't ever tell anyone else!"

"Finding the ancient stone was far more trouble than it was worth," Olof Ohman said, in Swedish. "That ugly, cursed rock ruined my life and the lives of my family. Don't let it do the same to you."

"If you don't mind being called a cheat and a fraud, you can tell the world. Your reputation will be destroyed as well. Finding that rock was the worst experience that ever happened to me in my life."

Upon returning to his home, the farmer unceremoniously unloaded the heavy, flat stones by dumping them from the hay wagon next to his house. He was building a cement foundation on his home and these stones would become a part of it.

Later, as he placed the stones in his basement foundation, he cemented them into place but with the writing facing outward so someone entering that part of his house could not see them. His family knew of them but they were never mentioned again.

The house has since been used as a granary and the basement has been filled in. The stones have remained there, underground and unnoticed, for nearly one hundred years.

Need books…

as gifts for family, students, friends or coworkers?

Copies of **The RUNESTONE** are available at:

Ralph Mayer
Fivecoats Publishing Company
31524 510th Ave.
Ottertail, Minnesota, 56571

Please send $14.95 (US), which includes $2.00 to cover shipping charges.

Signed copies are available upon request.